PUFFIN BOOKS

Vampire Stories to Tell in the Dark

Anthony Masters is well known as an adult and children's novelist, short-story writer and biographer. He has won the John Llewellyn Rhys Memorial Prize for his adult novel *The Seahorse*, and his recent children's book *Dead Man at the Door* (Puffin) was described by the *Sunday Telegraph* as 'A truly terrifying story, the fear of which is matched by the tension of the writing'. *The Times Educational Supplement* said of another children's novel *Spinner* (Blackie), 'This story succeeds because the action is compelling from the opening pages.'

He also spends much of his time working directly with children on his unique Book Explosion events on both sides of the Atlantic. These uniquely devised workshops bring together writing, drama games, mime, improvisation and adventure training.

He is married with three children and lives in Sussex.

Some other books by Anthony Masters

HORROR STORIES TO TELL IN THE DARK
SCARY TALES TO TELL IN THE DARK

DEAD MAN AT THE DOOR
PLAYING WITH FIRE
RAVEN
TRAVELLERS' TALES

Vampire Stories

to Tell in the Dark

Anthony Masters

PUFFIN BOOKS

PUFFIN BOOKS

Published by the Penguin Group
Penguin Books Ltd, 27 Wrights Lane, London W8 5TZ, England
Penguin Books USA Inc., 375 Hudson Street, New York, New York 10014 USA
Penguin Books Australia Ltd, Ringwood, Victoria, Australia
Penguin Books Canada Ltd, 10 Alcorn Avenue, Toronto, Ontario, Canada M4V 3B2
Penguin Books (NZ) Ltd, 182–190 Wairau Road, Auckland 10, New Zealand

Penguin Books Ltd, Registered Offices: Harmondsworth, Middlesex, England

Published in Puffin Books 1995
1 3 5 7 9 10 8 6 4 2

Typeset by Datix International Limited, Bungay, Suffolk
Filmset in 11/12 Monophoto Bembo

Printed in England by Clays Ltd, St Ives plc

Contents

'We shouldn't have come,' said Jon.

The crypt under the church was dark, but a security light glowed on the vault-shaped ceiling, illuminating two large, rather fearsome family memorials with grinning gargoyles at the top of the columns. There was a smell of shut-in dust and decay.

'We'll be OK.' Jodie was scoffing. 'Don't be so chicken. The warden's dead from the neck up.'

'That's what worries me,' Jon replied defensively. 'He looks like an off-duty vampire.'

Some of the others mumbled assent. They were all feeling uneasy, not knowing how to handle the situation. It had been Jodie who had dared them to leave the cosy safety of the youth hostel in the converted church and explore the crypt. The coast had been clear, as the warden and his wife were in their own quarters.

It was the dead of winter and the snow was gently falling outside in the city streets.

1

'Maybe we'll get snowed up and be in this place for days,' said Tom.

Jon shivered. 'How long are we going to be down here?'

'As long as it takes,' muttered Jodie.

'What does that mean?'

'As long as we dare.' She rounded on them. 'First one who goes back to the dormitory is a coward.'

No one moved, but their eyes shifted anxiously along the sombre plaques naming countless dead, to the darkened statues in the gloomy side-chapel — statues that looked as if they might come alive at any moment.

'What shall we do then?' asked Abby.

'We'll stay until dawn,' replied Jodie challengingly. 'And we'll tell stories.'

'What kind of stories?'

'How about vampire stories?' said Colin, fearfully looking round at the tombs. 'I bet this place is full of vampires.'

'Real-life vampires!' said Jodie. 'I've got one to tell first.'

Uneasily, the others sat down on the stone floor in front of the largest memorial of all.

'Anyone remember Tony Blake?' asked Jodie. 'That boy who left school to go to his parents' new sheep farm in Northumberland? He told me a really weird story before he went.'

1
Summer Pudding

Old Susan Parker was Tony Blake's 'summer friend'. Well into her seventies, she never left the house in winter and neither did her husband Matthew. The East Sussex countryside was remote and the old houses were swallowed up in small valleys. Susan and Matthew Parker had once kept a large herd of sheep and the local mystery was that they had all died off, one by one, until only one remained. Susan had explained to Tony that 'they had a wasting disease. Infected each other. No one could save 'em.' But he had never seen a vet visiting the farm.

Now the Parkers no longer farmed. They had sold all their land and never seemed to see anyone. Except Tony.

The Blakes were the Parkers' next-door neighbours, although they were separated by half a mile of woodland and could only be approached by what Tony's father called 'the old twisty track'. Tree roots stuck out of the banks on either side, and it was densely overhung with heavy branches. In winter Tony could just see the sky between the gnarled fingers of wood, but in the summer the leaves blotted out everything, making the lane permanently dark. When there was even the slightest wind the

3

trees rustled and sighed menacingly, but Tony refused to be put off, and when the days were longer he often visited his 'summer friend'.

He was a lonely boy, partly because his father's sheep farm was so far away from the school and the village, and partly through choice. A dreamer, Tony was close to the moods of the countryside, and in the holidays he liked to be alone, living the stories of the old days told to him by old Susan. Fascinated by her reminiscences, he liked to imagine that he was part of them. His visits to the Parkers' house would always have been a treat – if it hadn't been for the figure he thought he occasionally saw at Susan's upstairs window.

Tony had summoned up his courage and asked Susan if there was anyone up there, but she was cheerfully quick to deny it. 'Lord bless you, Tony, there's nothing up there but dust. I never get to the upstairs rooms with my rheumatics, and Mr Parker could never make them stairs with his arthritis. It's all shut off. Maybe you saw the curtain move in the breeze. There's a broken window up there that we'll never be able to fix.'

But when Tony suggested that his father could come and put in a new pane of glass, Susan was unhappy. 'We're too old to have strangers round.'

'You've got me.'

She smiled an old weather-beaten smile, which lit up her wrinkled brown face, and he looked at her affectionately. Susan Parker was small and hunched, but despite her rheumatism she was still physically strong, with her big hands and muscular arms.

'You're different. You're my summer friend. And you know what I've got for you today?'

'Summer pudding?'

'That's my boy.'

4

Susan would always bring the pudding out and put it down on the old moss-and-lichen-stained table in the overgrown front garden. She never allowed him inside the house.

This time the pudding was better than ever – a truly delicious concoction of crustless, thin white bread soaked with raspberries, redcurrants, blackcurrants and cherries. The pudding was a deep, gleaming red and Tony relished every succulent mouthful.

That was the day she told him their last sheep had died. 'Not that we need the living now. We've both got our pensions and the house is ours.'

'What did the vet say?' He looked at her, the last remnants of the pudding still clinging to his lips. Tony knew she'd never called the vet out in her life, but he also wanted to find out why.

'Nothing.'

'Why?'

'Nothing *to* say. It's a wasting disease. Like the rest of 'em.'

'What did they waste away from?'

But she quickly changed the subject. 'Now – how about some home-made lemonade to round off that pud?'

'Great.' The lemonade was almost as good as the pudding and Tony couldn't wait to be given a mugful of the glorious golden liquid. It was very hot in the garden and the insects seemed to be making an abnormal amount of noise. He had a slight headache and there was sweat on his brow. He was also acutely conscious of being watched.

The next few days were full of torrential rainstorms and wind, so when he started off on the first clear morning to the Parkers' house, the old twisty track was waterlogged and the saturated leaves overhead dripped, ice cold, on to his thin T-shirt.

There was a curious stillness to the old house as Tony emerged from the sodden foliage, and to his concern he saw that the dirty dish that had contained the summer pudding and the lemonade glass were still on the garden table. Then he caught sight of Susan Parker, sprawled face-down on the path. She looked like a rag doll, empty somehow, and even smaller.

Tony ran towards her, sure that she was dead, his heart pounding and the tears stinging at the back of his eyes. She must have lain there for days and she was soaked. Soaked and wasted. Wasted? Tony stood stock still. There was a limpness to her, a gathering of flesh in folds, a trace of blood, a general collapse. Her muscular arms were thin and drained.

Tony knew that he would have to go into the house. He pushed open the door into the dank interior, and very slowly his eyes became used to the darkness. There was a small hallway which smelt stale and musty, a short corridor, a flight of stairs, and beyond those a dining-room.

Tony paused. Wasn't that a step he had just heard? Breathing? He froze, staring up the staircase to the tiny landing. Was that a dark shadow moving? He shivered, squinting upwards through the gloom; there wasn't much light coming in through the small windows.

He forced himself on towards the dining-room, where, on the table, there was a large dish containing the last few crumbs of what Tony knew had been a summer pudding. Then he saw Matthew Parker.

Like his wife he was lying on his front, his limbs splayed out, his body curiously limp and drained. There was a small puncture mark on the back of his neck and a smear of blood on the floor. Tony stood there, horrified, unable to move, rooted to the spot as if he had entered into the fairy-tale spell of some bewitched cottage. How had they died? Had something attacked them? An animal? A dog? But they hadn't been savaged.

Then he heard another step on the stair. And another. Something, someone, was coming down. He could smell a fetid animal-like scent and caught the unmistakable sound of heavy breathing.

Then the steps stopped – and there was a silence.

'Who's there?' whispered Tony.

The silence intensified.

'Who's there?' he cried out a little louder. Then he heard the stairs creaking and the steps returning slowly upwards. Seizing his opportunity he ran out of the dining-room, down the passage, through the tiny hall and out into the warmth of the slowly strengthening sunshine. It was a glorious moment, dispersing his terror, comforting Tony as he stepped back into a more familiar world.

Two weeks passed. The inquest on the Parkers' deaths found that they had wasted away, presumably catching a disease from their sheep that neither vets nor doctors could diagnose.

The puncture on the back of Mr Parker's neck was explained away as a horsefly bite, as was a similar mark on his wife's throat. As to the steps on the staircase, the old house was searched and reported to be empty.

The long summer days continued and Tony felt very lonely. He no longer enjoyed his own company, for he missed old Susan deeply. Only once had he ventured down the twisty track, staying amongst the trees, noticing how quickly the already overgrown garden was creeping up the walls of the house, rather as if the natural world was claiming the place as its own.

Tony began to brood, and to cheer him up his parents gave him a Labrador puppy which he called Clover, but soon after the little dog's arrival, the Blakes' sheep began to suffer from the same wasting disease as the Parkers'. Bearing in mind what had happened to the old couple, the vet gave instructions that while tests were run the flock must be quarantined off in one field, only to be approached by Mr Blake wearing protective clothing.

Under strict instructions not to go anywhere near the field, Tony took Clover in the opposite direction, setting off down the old twisty track. His intention had been to stay in the woods, but as it was a bright afternoon he decided to take another look at the old house.

Tony gazed at it sadly, for a complete air of desolation hung over the place. Soon, he supposed, it would become a ruin. Then he had the eerie feeling of being watched and his eyes were drawn to the upstairs window. A surge of panic gripped him: he was certain he had seen a face.

This is crazy, he thought. The police had definitely checked to make sure no one was there and he knew the house had been put up for sale by a distant cousin. Then he saw the 'For Sale' sign. It was lying in the undergrowth, half covered with leaf mould.

Tony glanced furtively up at the window again, aware that Clover was keeping close to him.

'It's all right,' Tony whispered, ruffling her fur. But the puppy was growling now.

Boldly he went to the gate, while Clover hung back. Through the long grasses he could see the summer pudding plate and the empty lemonade glass, now covered in mould. A small piece of pudding was still there, and a wisp of lemon rind.

He stared up at the first-floor window, conscious

again of being watched, and saw, for a fraction of a second, a head that was quickly withdrawn. The shock jangled through his body. Then Tony noticed that the front door of the old house was slightly ajar.

Clover began to sniff the air, pointing her nose directly at the door and scuffing her paws in a way that Tony had seen before. This is what she normally did when she was hungry. Then, without warning, the puppy was off, forgetting her fear and dashing through the grass and thistles and overgrown hollyhocks to the front door. She pushed her way in, and with a joyous bark disappeared from view.

Tony stood outside indecisively. The last thing he wanted to do was go in after Clover, but he couldn't let the puppy run into danger. He looked up at the window again. There was no movement at all. Surely it was all in his imagination, he reasoned.

Cautiously, Tony edged through the door and went inside. The house was even more musty. Then he was practically knocked off his feet by a wildly excited Clover who, evading his outstretched arms, dived up the stairs with a friendly bark.

Knowing it would be useless to call her, Tony slowly mounted the stairs, sweating all over and shaking so much that he could hardly put one foot after the other.

Eventually he came to the landing. He had expected it to be thick with dust, but it was in fact quite clean, and he suddenly realized that the stairs looked as if they had been swept as well. Why was that? He paused and then forced himself on, hearing Clover scrabbling at something in the adjoining room and giving little barks of excitement.

Tony opened the door to a child's dilapidated nursery with a bed on one side, a cot on the other and a frieze of rabbits running around the sides of the room. There were a few old toys, including a huge, battered teddy bear and a soldier who had lost an arm. On a table in the centre were the remains of a summer pudding that Clover was gleefully finishing.

Hurriedly, Tony went over to the plate. The pudding looked slightly different, its juices an unnatural, brilliant red. Shrugging, he walked over to a huge cupboard which ran the length of the room, with an old sign over the top saying GREGORY PARKER'S TOY CUP-BOARD. PRIVATE. KEEP OUT. For a ghastly moment Tony thought he could hear breathing inside, but when he held his own breath to listen, he couldn't hear it any more.

Grabbing Clover, still feverishly eating, he carried her, struggling, downstairs, but as he reached the hall-way, the puppy jumped out of his arms and ran towards the kitchen.

The big, scrubbed wooden table in the centre held another half-finished summer pudding on which Clover was gorging herself. Against a side wall was a long, low freezer which was emitting a low hum. Why was it on, wondered Tony, when the house was meant to be up for sale? He looked out of the window to see a cable leading from the nearby pylon into the wall. Yes – that was it. Squatters had moved in. Tony breathed a sigh of relief and, leaving Clover to continue her feast, walked idly over to take a look in the freezer.

He gasped. It wasn't possible. Inside the freezer were dozens of huge summer puddings, wrapped individually in clingfilm, each gleaming blood-red in the hard artifi-cial light. What were they doing in there? Who were they for? Then he saw the note pasted on the underside of the lid. It read:

Matthew – the puddings are not up to strength since the last sheep died. I have contributed to this last batch. This is a reminder to be brave – to feed your son when I am gone. Your beloved Susan.

Tony stood there, his mind reeling. Slowly he came to an appalling conclusion. Then he heard the steps on the stairs.

Grabbing Clover yet again, Tony hurtled out of the kitchen without daring to glance up the stairs. He tore out of the door, through the overgrown garden and back on to the twisty track. He didn't stop running until he was outside his own house. Putting Clover down, he walked into the calm of his mother's big, clean, farmhouse kitchen, the puppy following at his heels.

'Mum –'

'What's up? You been running? Chasing that dog?'

'Did the Parkers ever have a son?'

'Well –' His mother seemed reluctant to answer.

'I *must* know.'

'She always made me promise I'd never tell anyone. Not that it would have mattered much, with her and Matthew such recluses. Do you know, I don't think they saw a soul in years. Except for your visits, they never –'

'Mum!' He was beside himself with impatience.

'All right. All right. Yes – they did. But sadly he suffered some kind of brain damage when he was young. I think he fell off a tractor. Anyway, he had to be put in an institution, apparently.'

'Are you sure?'

'Well, that's what she said. By the way, I'm doing something special for you. It won't be as good as Mrs Parker's. She was a *real* expert. But I've made a summer pudding for you.'

'Wow!' said Jon. 'Was he ever caught?'

'*I think so,*' *replied Jodie.*

'*You* think *so.*' *He looked nervously round the crypt.*

'*My cousin Alan had a nasty experience in Bulgaria last year,*' *said Jon.* '*That's why I don't like being down here. Of course, I didn't believe what he said — not a word. He's always making things up.*' *He paused.* '*Do you want to hear?*'

2
Buried Alive

Alan's mother is Bulgarian and she met his father while she was working as an au pair girl in London. She never talked about Stedok, the village she came from, hardly ever mentioned her parents and seemed happy never to go back to her country again.

Several times Alan and his dad had suggested a holiday there, but she always turned the idea down, so it was very much to their surprise that Margot said that she was going back to Stedok for her father's funeral. The return coincided with one of his dad's business trips, and when Alan asked her if he could go with her she at first refused. But by keeping on, he wore his mother down and she reluctantly agreed that he could accompany her.

She seemed tense on the plane, but when they arrived in Stedok she was more relaxed. Alan wasn't. Directly he saw the village he was uneasy: it seemed both brooding and hostile. There was one main street which straggled on into a huge agricultural plain, a few residential roads which also petered out into the vast, grey wheatfields, a closed-down cinema, a small motel, and an Orthodox church full of icons, surrounded by a large graveyard with the most ornate tombs and rusty railings.

But, although she was grieving, his grandmother was welcoming and Alan soon noticed how happy his mother was in the little stucco-fronted house with its vegetable garden, old-fashioned television and collections of icons and dolls in traditional costume.

The funeral was a big one, with most of the villagers lining the route to the graveyard, the coffin being carried in a black funeral carriage pulled by two black horses wearing purple plumes. After the service, it was borne out to the magnificent family tomb in the graveyard and placed on a stone shelf inside.

As they were leaving the graveyard, his mother introduced Alan to a cousin, a young girl named Sojit, who was the most beautiful person he had ever met in his life. She had a graceful, willowy figure and her dark hair fell thickly on to a long, milky-skinned neck.

'Your grandfather was a fine old man, kind and good. The end of a long line. Thank God,' Sojit said.

'What do you mean – thank God?'

She looked awkward, as if she had accidentally said the wrong thing, but however hard he tried Alan couldn't get out of Sojit what she really meant.

That night, tucked up in a hard little bed in a small, box-like room, Alan had the most awful nightmare. He dreamt that he had been buried alive and was knocking at the side of his coffin in a desperate attempt to get someone to come and release him. But no one came, the air inside grew thinner and the lid was unyielding. He knew he was going to die.

Suddenly he woke up, sweating, not sure where he was. He looked up at the low ceiling and fancied the walls were closing in on him. It was as if he was still buried alive. There was a sound too – the urgent sound of someone knocking on wood.

Gradually Alan came to, realizing that he was spending the first night in his Bulgarian room. He wasn't in a coffin; he was in bed – but what was that knocking?

It was definitely coming from outside, and every moment it seemed to increase in sound and volume. There was a terrible urgency to it. Someone, somewhere, must be trapped and desperately trying to attract attention.

Alan jumped out of bed and opened his window. It was a late September night and he could smell autumn in the air. There was the pungent aroma of damp earth.

The sound of knocking increased. It seemed to come from the graveyard. Why hadn't anyone else heard it, he wondered. Then he saw that at least one other person had – a slim figure was opening a side gate over the road and running furtively along the shadowed side of the street. Sojit.

As he crept out of his grandmother's house, Alan found that the knocking sound was doubling, trebling, quadrupling, until it became a terrifying din. Why had no one else heard this racket except for him and Sojit? But where was she now?

Hurriedly, he followed the sound to the graveyard. Because of the size of the monuments, the carved pillars and massive cupolas, the decorated arches and cathedral-like roofs, the graveyard looked more like a city, picked out in minute detail by the hard, silver moonlight.

And the knocking was still increasing in volume and urgency.

As Alan ran over the tussocky grass, he wondered where Sojit had gone. He rapidly increased his pace. Gradually his fear ebbed away – he was beginning to experience a glorious sensation of wellbeing and happy anticipation.

Then he found her.

Sojit was lying over a small grave, and Alan could see that she had gashed her cheek. A small trickle of bright-red blood was flowing, made more pronounced by the sharp, clear moonlight. Her long, pale neck was partly covered by a scarf and she was not unconscious – just stunned and already stirring slightly.

'Who's that?' Sojit moaned.

'It's Alan. Are you hurt?'

'I don't know. What are you doing here? You shouldn't be here!' She became frantic.

'I heard the knocking. But it's stopped. That's odd.'

'We must go home now.'

'But what was all that noise?'

'It was in your imagination.'

'Rubbish!'

'We must go, Alan.' Shakily, Sojit staggered to her feet and then, with a little cry, touched the blood on her cheek. Suddenly she was terribly afraid.

'There's blood on your cheek,' said Alan. 'But it's drying –'

'Keep away!' She darted away from him.

Alan couldn't drag his eyes from the blood on her cheek. Even now there was a glorious bright-red drop rolling down. He was suddenly thirsty, and a voice in his head told him to drink. Alan advanced on Sojit and she drew back again, this time with a harsh cry of fear.

Then the knocking began again, just as urgent as before.

'Can you hear that?' he asked.

'Yes.'

'Why doesn't anyone else come?'

'Because *they* can't hear. Let's go. Now!'

'So it's just us two then,' said Alan. 'Why's that?' But there was something dawning in his mind; it was so horrific that he couldn't possibly think about it. Not now. Not here.

The knocking continued, growing even louder than before.

'Don't follow it,' Sojit implored. 'Come home with me.'

But a yearning as strong and compulsive as the strange feeling he had had when he saw Sojit's blood came over Alan, and he knew that he must go.

The mausoleum was very ornate, with its iron railings and painted wood and icons inlaid into the arched pillars. The bronze door looked firmly shut, but when Alan rattled the handle it opened slowly towards him on rusty hinges. Directly he was inside, the knocking sound stopped and there was absolute silence. Could he have imagined it all? Was he still dreaming? Sleepwalking?

Gradually Alan's tension drained away, and although it was unpleasantly spooky in the mausoleum he was not afraid – just tired and rather irritable. The stone monuments were dusty and dirty-looking, and there was an unpleasant smell that was vaguely familiar. He looked around nervously, and at the very back of the vault he could just pick out a bunch of wild garlic. Next to it was a cross. The villagers had clearly tried to warn off the vampires, but obviously their thirst was too great.

The silence lengthened. Then he saw that his grandfather's shiny new coffin was open.

Eagerly, Alan walked over and peered into the casket. The thing inside had a livid white face and its claw-like hands were tightly gripping the sides.

'You are one of us, Alan.' The voice was dry as a husk.

'I don't understand.' He was finding it increasingly difficult to breathe and his chest was tight as a drum.

Then Alan saw the stone lids of the other tombs being pushed away by rotting fingers. Men with sallow, bloodless features were clambering out. One of them held up an icon – an image of a young woman with a long white neck.

'Where is the girl?'

'She's gone home,' said Alan quickly, too quickly.

'I smell blood, Alan.'

'I don't understand –'

'Oh, but you do. You are one of us. One of the line. You're family. My last male descendant. And you are thirsty. Where is she?'

But Sojit was already standing by the open mausoleum, brave and defiant. 'I'm going home now, Alan. Please come with me.'

Alan looked at the lily-white neck. 'You go,' he said. 'I'll follow . . .'

'I don't believe you, Jon,' said Mary.

'That's up to you.' Jon grinned strangely. It was difficult to know what he was thinking.

Mary turned hurriedly away.

'I used to have horrible dreams about the baby-sitter we had when we lived in America,' said Joanna. 'Would you like to hear the whole story?'

3
The Sitter

We used to live in New England. Actually it's more like Norway than England, with remote, rolling countryside, thickly wooded hills and clapboard houses half hidden amongst the trees. The local community was isolated and there had been rumours of witchcraft in the last century.

At that time, my brother Zak and I were often looked after by sitters while our parents went out to dinner or the theatre. Our father was doing a five-year stint with an American insurance company and they were often asked out for business entertainment, so they were always hunting for good sitters.

But Zak and I used to resent being in this house miles from anywhere. There was no one to play with and we were too dependent on each other. He's five years older than me and didn't want to play with a boring baby sister and I didn't want to have anything to do with a rough idiot of a brother.

So we took it out on the sitters, and gave them hell. They didn't stay long. One of them tripped over a piece of tightly stretched black nylon and broke her ankle, and an older one, Ellie Harbottle – well, we put glue on the toilet seat, and she really got stuck. Dad was furious.

Then one weekend he said he'd found absolutely the right person in the nearby town of Salem. Apparently she was known to be quiet, strict and determined – her name was Carrie Hewlett. I have to say that from that moment on we viewed her as a challenge.

Carrie was a bit of a shock when she came. She was small and young, but she wore a sober dress, dark cardigan, grey stockings and flat, sensible shoes. Her hair was done up into a bun and her face had that well-scrubbed look. She smelt of soap and washing-powder.

'I want to make one thing clear to you guys,' she said as she plumped down on the sofa and got out some knitting. 'You give me trouble and I'll get your dad to lambaste you.'

Neither Zak nor I knew what lambaste meant – but it didn't sound too good. What was worse, Dad had been getting very tough recently, particularly since the sitters had been going down so fast. Maybe he would do what Carrie said.

'Shall I turn on the TV for you?' I asked, hoping to chat her up a bit and give her a false sense of security.

'Never watch it.'

'Do you mind if we do –'

'Sure I mind.'

'What?' asked Zak, amazed.

'Watching TV's a real bad thing to do. I've brought you some books to read.'

'I don't read books,' said Zak firmly.

'Not that kind anyway,' I told her, as she put two large volumes down on the table.

'Take your pick.' She smiled as if she had given us a real treat and resumed her knitting.

Both of the books looked deadly. One was called *One Hundred Uplifting Examples of Moral Heroism*, the other

Pastor Mustard Tells the Good News. We sat at the table, turning the pages and pretending that we were reading, but secretly plotting.

'Do you enjoy books like this?' asked Zak, trying to draw her out.

'Sure I do.' Her face was pale but radiant, and her big blue eyes were alive with enthusiasm.

'Where did you get them?' he persisted.

She smiled at him brightly. There was something nasty about that smile. For the first time in my life I was afraid of an adult. As for Zak, I knew by the fixed way he was looking at her that he was scared too.

'I got them from our library.'

'Your home library?'

'Oh no. The society's library.'

'What society is that?' I asked her curiously.

'The Society of Love.'

'Is that a Church?'

'No. It's a company of friends and believers.'

'What do you believe in?' asked Zak, and Carrie met his gaze with a cold, blue stare that seemed to penetrate right through him.

'Purity. Purity of spirit, of living, of behaving.'

I thought of all the bad things we'd done to the other sitters. We hadn't been very pure – and Carrie definitely wouldn't have approved.

'How does the society ... operate?' asked Zak more hesitantly.

'We meet and talk in our little wooden hall that's tucked right away in the woods. And we pledge ourselves to purity.'

'How do you do that?' I got in before Zak could ask another question. I frowned at him.

'We drink from the cup. There is only one direction. One life. We love little children because they are at their most pure.' Carrie gave me a special, strong, all-embracing smile. Then she turned to Zak and her smile snapped off. 'But of course, little children grow up and become corrupt.' She paused. 'Are you corrupt, Zak?'

'No,' he said virtuously. 'Not at all.'

Carrie looked away. Has she ever had any fun in her life, I thought. Has she ever been corrupt herself?

'Do you all drink from the cup?' Zak asked, ignoring my warning glance.

'When it's filled.'

Zak seemed fascinated by her flashing knitting-needles. They were going so fast that they were almost a blur.

'But what's it full of?'

She smiled again and we were almost mesmerized by her startling radiance. 'Why – the stuff of life, of course. Now you two should be in bed, shouldn't you?'

It was too early, but neither of us cared. We were only too glad to go upstairs and talk about her.

'She's awful.' Zak sat on the end of my bed.

'Keep your voice down,' I admonished him.

'We've got to get rid of her.'

'She'll be tricky.'

'But she's only a kid.' Zak was thoughtful. 'There must be a way –'

'She scares me.'

'Yes – she does me.'

I looked at him in amazement. He never admitted to weakness, so he *must* have been scared.

'What are we going to do then?'

My brother grinned, but the grin was shaky. 'We could scare the living daylights out of her. You can see she's led a sheltered life.'

'Be careful, Zak. There's something about her. That look.'

'You mean she's a nutter?'

'I mean she's tough.'

'Tough, eh?'

I couldn't have said a worse thing, because Zak loved a challenge. 'I wonder if she'd be tough enough to face up to a bit of a fright?'

'What kind of fright did you have in mind?'

'You know my cassette deck and speakers?'

'Yes.'

'You know I record on them.'

'Yes.' I was feeling very wary now.

'You know I've got that long extension lead –'

'Zak, you've got to be careful.'

'I've got a plan to scare old droopy drawers – out of her droopy drawers.'

As he began to explain I grew even more afraid. I was sure Zak didn't understand who he was taking on.

'Are you asleep?'

'Mm.' I was pretending to be.

Carrie stood in the doorway, a shawl over her shoulders, looking sallow but still bright-eyed. 'Shall I come in and tuck you up?'

'I'm OK.'

'Would you like a story? I know your brother wouldn't. He's too old.'

To cover up what I knew Zak was doing in the garden, I agreed to the story – just in case Carrie went and checked in his bedroom. She sat on the end of my bed and I smelt the sensible soap. For some reason the smell scared me.

'What would you like?'

'Er –' I was at a loss.

'A fairy story?'

'I suppose –'

'Or a poem? I'm rather partial to poems. Would you like to have a poem?'

'Yes – I'd love to hear a poem.'

'Very well. Let me see.' She tossed her head back, and then, to my amazement, began to sing a nursery rhyme.

> 'Ding, dong, bell, pussy's in the well.
> Who put her in? Little Johnny Green.
> Who pulled her out? Little Tommy Stout.
> What a naughty boy was that,
> To try to drown poor pussy cat,
> Who never did him any harm,
> And killed the mice in his father's barn.'

I listened dutifully, but as I listened I shivered. Carrie obviously hated boys. She was really strange.

'Does Zak persecute cats?'

'Oh no. He loves them.' I thought she looked rather disappointed, so I was determined to probe a bit more. 'Can I ask you a question about your society?'

'Of course,' she agreed readily, but I thought I caught a cautious look in her eye.

'Do you have boys in it?'

She shook her head and looked grim. 'Never. I think they're a waste of space, don't you?'

Suddenly I felt very sleepy. Carrie showed no signs of going away. How long was Zak going to be in the garden, I wondered.

My eyes closed despite my attempts to keep awake, and for a few moments I must have drifted off to sleep. When I awoke there was a sharp stinging on my neck. The room was dark, but I could hear Carrie singing and using the vacuum cleaner outside. What *was* this sting-ing? My hand went to my neck and in my horror I touched a substance that was sticky and red. Blood. I began to scream.

Carrie convinced me I'd dropped off to sleep and somehow lain on my comb. I often untangled my hair before going off to sleep and I suppose it was possible that I had made the pinpricks in my throat that way. I looked at the comb doubtfully – it seemed very blunt to me.

Carrie put a plaster on my neck and I felt better. Then I caught sight of a red stain on the carpet just outside my bedroom door.

'What's that stain?' I asked.

For the first time, Carrie looked uncomfortable. 'I dropped something. Guess I thought I'd vacuumed it all up.'

'You don't get rid of a stain with a vacuum.'

'No.' She was very much on the defensive and I instinctively pressed home the advantage.

'What did you drop?'

'Little jar of mine.'

'What was in it?'

'Some, er – some perfume. It was red.'

'Perfume? You wouldn't use perfume!' I was completely astounded. 'I mean perfume's corrupt, isn't it, by your book?'

'It belonged to my grandmother. Guess it's sentimental . . . Anyway, I'll get some stain remover and –'

Suddenly, a sinister, amplified voice came from the garden below.

'CARRIE HEWLETT – YOU OF THE PURE SOUL –'

She froze, turning towards the sound with wild eyes, as if the age of miracles had finally arrived and she was about to witness Armageddon – the end of the world.

'What's that?' she whispered.

'YE WHO HAVE LIVED FOR PURITY, HEAR THIS.'

Carrie flattened herself against the wall.

'YOU ARE THE CHOSEN ONE. YOU ARE TO BE OUR GUIDE. YOU MUST GO TO THAT GREAT CITY OF PURITY.'

I watched Carrie gradually move away from the wall, the suspicion growing in her eyes. Her suspicion turned to anger. Could she have recognized that amplified voice?

The music blared out without warning and the singer relentlessly proclaimed, 'NEW YORK, NEW YORK. IT'S A WONDERFUL TOWN.'

Carrie's eyes flashed with fury and she turned to me. 'Your brother –'

'Er –'

'It's your brother, isn't it?'

'It's only a joke.'

'Mocking me.'

'Just a joke!' I repeated.

'He'll mock me no longer!'

'What are you going to do?'

'Take him into the pit.'

'I don't know what you're talking about,' I said, trying to leap out of bed, but she gave me a hard shove that sent me flying back over the duvet.

'He *shall* be punished.'

'Don't hurt him.'

She smiled at me mockingly, but it was more like a snarl than a smile.

'Don't hurt him,' I whispered again. 'It was only a joke.'

She laughed, and when Carrie opened her mouth I could see her teeth. They were even and clean and white. But it was the one in the centre that terrified me.

The tooth was long and pointed and razor sharp. Her eyes burnt with a terrible longing.

I followed Carrie, but she ran like a gazelle, and I soon lost her in the wild part of the garden.

But then I heard Zak give a sudden cry – a cry of terrible fear. I came to an abrupt halt, frozen, trying to detect where he was, but realizing I had lost all sense of direction in the wilderness.

After what seemed ages I heard Carrie's voice howling with rage. 'You are corrupt,' she screamed. 'All boys are corrupt.' This was followed by the repeated sound of breaking and smashing and I knew she must be hitting his cassette deck against a tree. 'Now,' she said finally. 'Now.'

I knew she was going to attack Zak. There was no sound from him and I guessed he was rooted to the spot with fear.

But he must have made an amazing recovery because suddenly I could hear him running through the undergrowth, with Carrie howling like a banshee behind him. The noise of the chase continued, sometimes coming closer to me, sometimes dying away. Then there was a silence which lengthened and deepened. Had she caught him? Had Carrie strangled my brother? Or had he, by some miracle, got away?

Then I heard her voice, loud and commanding and vengeful. 'You will be punished,' she said.

And the silence returned.

I found Zak by a stream, unharmed but shaken. 'You OK?' he demanded.

'Yes.'

'What's that mark on your neck?'

'I went to sleep and lay on my comb,' I said. 'It cut me.'

'A comb wouldn't do that.'

'Carrie said it did.'

'Carrie would . . .' He paused, panting slightly, still trembling.

'Where is she?'

'Gone. Did you see her tooth?'

'Yes.'

'I thought she was going to attack me. She was in a furious temper. But she didn't touch me.'

'Why not?'

'She ran off.' Zak pointed at the dusty leaves of the white-flowered plants illuminated by the pale moonlight.

'I don't understand –'

'That stuff down there. It's wild garlic.'

'I still have the scar,' said Joanna. They had moved away from the tombs now and were huddled together in a corner on the cold stone floor.

'It's strange, isn't it?' said Jud. 'I had an experience I've never wanted to talk about, but I s'pose it's a bit similar. It happened at school actually. Are you going to share this with me, Alex?'

'Share?' asked Jon.

'We went to the same boarding-school, in Northumberland,' replied Alex. 'And we had this awful experience, didn't we? But neither of us has ever talked about it. We thought we'd be laughed at, and anyway, we were scared out of our minds. Maybe it'll help to talk about it now. Shall I start, Jud?'

4
Matron's Madness

The school stands high up on a cliff overlooking the North Sea, and we both remember it as being really bleak. My mother used to call it a 'Gothic pile' – it was a bit like a fortress, I suppose. But I used to think the tall, black, huddled buildings, which pointed to the sky, were like a big black crow, ready to take off over the wide dark sea.

It was actually hell being there. Jud and I soon found *that* out, and we'd only been there half a term. There were five hundred boys, all-male staff and the head a bachelor – a strange guy called A.A. Kimber. He was like a hawk, with his thin head and tall body and black gown. He told the parents the school was a 'much needed return to traditional values'. Well, the traditional values were cold showers, running down the cliff paths – and up again, with the gym master behind you – freezing dormitories, bad food, and a fine view of the sea.

Anyway, the awful experience started when we got a new matron. Her name was Jane Dixon and she was very young and pretty. The staff made her feel at home at once, partly because they liked her and partly because the head couldn't keep any matrons at all. They kept leaving, and the rumour was that he fancied them and made their lives difficult.

Shortly after Jane Dixon came to the school I was doing a bit of exploring and discovered that A.A. Kimber had one of the biggest and most interesting wine-cellars I'd ever seen – much better than my father's, and his is fantastic. He's a connoisseur. I've always liked the taste of wine and thought Jud, my best friend, should be introduced to it too. So, one afternoon when we were both recovering from colds and were off games, I led him down to the cellar.

I was just looking for a place to dispose of a half-empty bottle we'd drunk, when I discovered a crate of about forty bottles, all unlabelled, at the back. In the light of a torch we had found in an alcove, we could see that they contained a bright-red liquid. We both guessed that it was tomato juice, probably used when the Bishop of Baxbury turned up. He's the chairman of the governors and a well-known teetotaller, who's always banging on in his sermons about the 'evils of drink'.

'I'll take over now, Alex,' said Jud. And he continued . . .

That wine was good, so Alex and I used to nip down quite regularly to sample the headmaster's claret. Now, there's something about Alex I know he won't mind me telling you. He may be curious and nosy, but he's not so good at observing people, and it's here that I score. For instance, I saw that our new matron was getting a little nervous and that A.A. Kimber always seemed to be 'checking on' or 'supervising' something or other in the sick-bay. And Matron was also worried by the large number of boys who kept coming to her looking pale and washed out. One of them told me that

Jane Dixon was giving them iron tablets to try and pep them up a bit.

Then I happened to overhear the head inviting her to dinner in his flat in the annexe. 'Just a small tête-à-tête,' he told her. 'So we get to know each other – and our working practices.'

I happened to be hanging around the cellar, waiting to see if the coast was clear for a gulp or two, when I saw old Conger, one of the head's cronies who often hung around the school, staggering down the steps. I hid in an alcove and watched him go in and come out with two bottles of the tomato juice. I didn't know if Jane Dixon was teetotal or not, but I certainly knew A.A. Kimber drank like a fish. So it seemed weird just to have tomato juice for their first cosy dinner together.

Jane Dixon was right to be nervous of A.A. Kimber. There was something about this long, lean stick of a man that really gave me the creeps. He seemed to get on well with some of the boys and they often went to his flat for tea, but I knew he disliked me, and several times he kept me in detention after his Latin class. He was mean-minded to the boys who weren't his pets – and too kind to the ones who were. Worse still, the boys who were unpopular with A.A. Kimber were usually unpopular with certain other members of staff – mainly those who had been there for a long time.

I also felt sorry for Jane Dixon. She was all right, really warm and caring. She didn't deserve a dinner party with Kimber, but it would be interesting to see how their cosy evening went.

In the light of all this, Alex and I decided to spy on Kimber's session with Jane Dixon by creeping up his back garden and getting a quick squint through the window. Alex knew from a previous surveillance that one curtain didn't quite close in the lounge – and would give us a reasonable view of cocktail time at least.

When we got there we were in luck. Not only was it a hot summer night, not only was the curtain still not fitting, but the window was also ajar so we could hear as well as see.

The rather dingy lounge, with its heavy oak furniture and funereal-looking sideboard, had only one shaded light in operation. On the central table were some sickly-looking cyclamens and a tray of drinks, which included a bottle of vodka and two large bottles of the tomato juice. Not a teetotal evening then!

A.A. Kimber was dressed in a hideous sports jacket with leather patches on the elbows, flannels and the school tie, with a crest and Latin motto which translated as 'BE NOT FAINTHEARTED'. He was like a gaunt, grey giraffe as he hovered over Jane Dixon, who was sitting in an armchair, looking awkward and nervous.

'I'm so pleased to have you on our staff, my dear,' the head was saying in his thin, slightly nasal voice.

'Thank you.'

'Your youth makes a big difference to staff *and* boys. Your youth and enthusiasm and – if I may so – dedication.'

'There's something I'd like to mention,' she said hesitantly.

'Yes?'

'It very much concerns me how many boys are suffering from anaemia. It's really quite serious.'

'But you know we do specialize in providing education for some delicate boys here.'

'Yes, I realize that, but have you ever had the situation investigated?'

32

'Investigated?'

'Yes. The medical officer of health. A visit can be arranged.'

'I'm sure there's no need.' Kimber paused. 'And now – will you have a cocktail?'

'Well –'

'Vodka and tomato juice?'

'I don't usually –'

'Just tomato juice perhaps?'

'Well –' She was hesitant.

'I'd like you to try this. It's a little hobby of mine.'

'You make it personally?'

'From the tomatoes in my greenhouse – with the addition of some herbs. It's very nutritious.'

'Yes. I'd love to try some.'

With a smile, he poured out a generous quantity into her glass and then mixed himself a large vodka and tomato juice. '*Santé*,' he said.

'Cheers,' she replied.

Then A.A. Kimber gave grunt of annoyance. 'That window –'

'Window?'

'The curtain's come off its runners . . .'

He came towards the window. We fled.

Just before lights-out Alex and I went to the boys' toilet on the ground floor, hoping to see Jane Dixon returning to her own quarters in the school. After a while she came through the back door. We had expected to see her hunted-looking, alarmed, fed up, angry – instead she looked happy and contented. We just couldn't get over it. What had happened? She couldn't have *liked* Kimber, could she? The very thought was impossible. We were completely thrown – and that's why we got caught.

'Bilson and Timberlake – what do you think you're

doing skulking behind that door?' Her tone was quite different: sharp and impatient and horribly like Kimber's. 'Go back to the dormitory immediately. It's after lights-out. I shall report you to the headmaster.'

We ran back up the stairs and managed to get into bed before the prefects came round. But we had the feeling that she *would* report us, and wondered why. She didn't seem to be the same person any more.

'I'll tell the last part, Jud,' said Alex.

It was me who woke up and heard the sounds of crying. Getting out of bed I saw Jimmy Brunson quivering under his duvet. He was the nervous type, often home-sick and very pale. In fact, he was the only boy in our dormitory who was.

'What's up?'

'Nothing,' Jimmy snivelled.

'Come on –'

'I'm scared.'

'Why?'

'Can't tell.'

'What are you scared about?' I asked angrily, realizing I was making him afraid of me now. 'I want to help you,' I persisted.

'You can't,' he replied hopelessly. Then he seemed to change his mind and began to speak quickly and desperately. 'Old Kimber and the others – they make us give blood. We're all the same blood group, you see – it's Group B – but I'm the only one in this dorm.'

'What?' I stared at him unbelievingly. 'You can't be serious –'

'I am. We have a blood test directly we get into school. Don't you remember?'

'Well – yes.' I remembered all right, but at the time

I'd thought it was just a routine part of the school medical records. 'They can't make you do that. You've got to go to the police.'

'They wouldn't believe me.' There was a depressing certainty to his voice. 'They're coming.' Jimmy was terrified. 'They're *all* coming. Go back to bed. Fast.'

'I can't hear anyone.'

'I can feel them. I can feel them already. *Please* go back to bed.'

'Why hasn't *anyone* – any of the other boys – tried to report what's going on?'

'Because they drink.'

'Drink what?' This was ridiculous, but I could hear the footsteps on the thinly carpeted stairs now, so I dashed over and quickly woke up Jud.

'There's something really odd going on,' I said. 'I think –' But I was interrupted.

On the threshold was A.A. Kimber, his eyes alight with pleasure. Behind him, holding a candle, was Jane Dixon, followed by four or five masters and a crowd of older boys. Then Jimmy gave a snivelling cry, and Kimber and Jane Dixon began to walk towards him, drawing back their lips.

Seconds later, Jud and I had thrown open the window and were shinning down the drainpipe. No one attempted to stop us. They were all too intent on the task in hand.

'Of course, no one ever believed us,' said Jud.

Sarah stood up. 'I can't stand much more of this. I'm going back to bed.'

'On your own?' asked Alex. 'Into that big, empty dormitory on your own?'

'I've never been able to live with my experiences as easily as you two did,' Sarah said suddenly. 'I've never been able to talk about it. Now I suppose it might be different.'

5
The Mounds

Most years, we went for our holidays in France, staying in houses well off the beaten track. It was always just the three of us – me and my parents. My father is a priest and my mother a nurse and we loved our precious times together. Some of my friends would say 'Fancy going on holiday with just your parents – that must be incredibly boring,' and although I told them it wasn't, they never believed me.

The year I remember in particular, we went to the Loire. The countryside felt remote, with the huge meandering river, sandy river-beaches, and small towns.

Our house was just outside a village, square and stone-built, with flaked paint shutters, and a well in the paved courtyard. At the very back of the walled garden there were these mounds. They looked like graves, and they were. Dogs' graves, according to the estate agent. The odd thing was that it looked as if no grass had ever grown over the cracked, hard earth. 'It must be the climate,' said my father, and dismissed the curiosity from his mind. For some reason, I couldn't.

The agents said the house had only just come on to the market for letting, was owned by an old lady called Angelique Dubois and had originally been lived in by

her daughter and her husband, Marie and André Benoit.
When my parents inquired about them in the local
charcuterie, the shopkeeper changed the subject quite
pointedly and discussed the weather instead, in what I
thought was a more British than French way.

Next day, I decided to have a look round the village
while my parents sat reading in the garden. I always like
to walk around places on my own, because I can drink
in the atmosphere and get the feel of the community.
There was a small church, a couple of shops in the
rundown square, a closed-up village school and one
single, lonely-looking petrol-pump. Chickens ran everywhere and there was a farmyard smell, even in the
graveyard that was jam-packed with ancient tombstones,
all leaning over at crazy angles.

I strolled back through the square, feeling rather
thirsty. It was near midday and I thought I'd pop into
the village shop and buy a cold drink. But directly I
tried to open the door, it was slammed and locked
against me. I stared through the glass questioningly at
the madame, who shrugged and turned away. I looked
at my watch. Ten to twelve. Did she normally close this
early? Oh well, I thought, I'll have the drink at home.

Feeling slightly vexed but nothing more, I strolled
past the petrol-pump and saw an old woman, clad in
layers of cardigans and with black stockings, sitting on a
wooden chair. She had her eyes closed, but when I
passed she opened them and gave me a strange sign,
holding up her thumb and forefinger and making them
into the shape of an O. Then she crossed herself and
looked away. Sweating now, I hurriedly headed for
home.

'Dad.'

He was in a deckchair, wearing a white linen jacket

and an old panama hat. My father seemed reassuringly the same – the Englishman abroad. I loved him for it.

He looked up and gave me a sweet, slow smile. 'Had a good walk? Mum's in the kitchen – producing something delicious.'

'Have you been to the village?'

'Not yet.'

'I tried to get a drink in the shop, but she shut the door in my face.'

'They always observe the siesta.' He yawned, wanting one himself.

'And there's an old lady by the petrol-pump who gave me a funny sign.' I repeated it to Dad, feeling rather idiotic as I did so. But he didn't laugh.

'I see.'

'Is something wrong?'

He looked concerned. 'Did she cross herself afterwards?'

'Yes.'

'She gave you the evil eye, then.'

'What's that supposed to mean?' I asked indignantly.

'It's just an old custom.'

'What kind of old custom?' I persisted, wondering why he was being so evasive.

'It's to guard against Satan and the supernatural.'

'Great.'

'But she only gave it to you because you're a stranger. They're very superstitious round here. Anyway – I bet you the old lady's bonkers.'

For some reason I didn't think so.

'What a pong,' said Mum that evening, as we sat out in the courtyard listening to the noise of the grasshoppers rubbing their feet together.

It was odd. Darkness had fallen; it had been a hot day and I could smell herbs and wild flowers. But all that was overlaid by a foul smell – something dead? The buried dogs? Surely they couldn't smell like this – they'd been under the ground far too long for that. But there was a smell all right, and when I walked down to the cracked and sun-baked earth of the mounds the smell got worse. Much worse.

My father stood beside me, sniffing. 'That's drains.'

'There aren't any, are there?' I asked.

'Cesspit then.'

'We're not on one,' said Mum, coming up. 'There's a septic tank and it's quite OK. I've just checked.'

'It must be something buried,' said my father reflectively.

'Which only smells at night?' I asked. 'It certainly wasn't smelling down here in the heat.'

'Must be some kind of herb that sends off a scent in the evening then.'

'Some scent,' said Mum.

I shivered. The night suddenly seemed cold.

For some reason I woke about three and found the atmosphere of my room stiflingly hot. The contrast with the previous night was startling. I went to the window and flung wide the shutters, only to see the two mounds sharply etched in the moonlight. Both were cracked open.

Should I get my parents? Should I go down there first and check them out? Maybe it was just a trick of the moonlight. Something inside me was insisting that I should go and find out by myself.

A cold wind blew through the scrubby garden as I walked slowly down towards the mounds. The change in temperature made me feel exposed and deeply apprehensive, but the smell seemed to have gone.

Eventually I stood beside the mounds in my dressing-gown, looking down with a mixture of fear and curiosity. They had cracked open at the top and earth had been flung everywhere, but when I peered into them I could only see darkness. Then I heard the click.

The small gate in the garden wall had closed. Immediately the awful smell returned and I froze. The gate was just behind me and I didn't want to turn round.

The disgusting smell increased. Was that a cough I heard? I didn't want to find out, so I raced for the house, running lightly up the stairs and back into my room. I closed the shutters quickly and huddled under the bedclothes until merciful, exhausted sleep eventually came.

In the morning, the mounds were back to normal. There was no sign of disturbance and no smell. I felt tired but fairly calm.

'Quite a crowd up at the churchyard this morning,' said my father. 'Apparently some graves were desecrated last night.'

'How awful.' Mum was horrified.

'Terrible.' I was very taken aback and remembered the click of the latch last night, as well as the all-pervasive smell. I had almost put it down to a dream – but not when I saw the dusty earth on my slippers. Should I tell them now, or would they think I was being idiotic? I decided to wait.

'There are some policemen up there – and the local priest. They were all very upset.' Dad turned to me. 'You'll be interested to know I got the evil eye too this morning.'

'From the police?' I stuttered.

Dad smiled. 'From the old lady. But the priest *did* have something to say to me: he wondered if we'd been disturbed last night.'

'Who by?'

'The vandals, I suppose.'

That was the time I should have told them everything, but for some reason I just couldn't.

Later that morning, when my parents were in the house, I went down to have a look at the mounds again. They were completely undisturbed, so I decided to walk up to the churchyard.

When I arrived, the police had gone and no one was around, but I could see that the wrought-iron gate of a large mausoleum had been smashed in and a stone sarcophagus had been dragged out of the vault.

'*Bonjour.*'

The priest was emerging from the Romanesque church. He was small and thin and spiky-looking.

'*Bonjour,*' I replied in a crashingly bad accent. '*Comment ça va?*' I realized I was probably being too familiar and stopped in confusion, turning red and no doubt looking extremely stupid.

'You are the little Carter girl?' he said, switching to his good English.

'Yes.'

'In the Benoit house?'

'That's right. I'm sorry to hear about the vandals,' I remarked uncertainly, wondering if he would open up.

'A terrible occurrence. Terrible.' He looked at me closely. 'There was a dreadful smell at the mausoleum this morning.'

'Smell?'

'Yes, of – putrefaction. Do you understand what I mean?'

'Yes,' I replied uneasily. I understood all too well.

'Do you *know* the smell I mean? You may have noticed it elsewhere?' he probed.

'Yes. In my – our – the back garden. There are two mounds.'

'Ah.' He smiled strangely. 'Do you mind if I walk back to your house with you? We need to arrange an exorcism.' His words sent a chill through me.

We walked back through the village, passing the old lady by the petrol-pump. But she gave me no evil eye, looking humbly down at the pavement.

'Marie and André Benoit used to live in the house you are staying in. It is my belief their love was forged in hell.' The priest spoke seriously, with great sadness.

'What did they do?' I asked.

'Terrorized the village.'

'In what way?' I persisted, determined to get him to tell me everything.

He didn't answer for what seemed like ages. Then he said unhappily, looking away from me, 'They liked to drink blood.'

'You mean they were –'

'I'd prefer not to use the word. Eventually they were – dealt with by the community.'

'You mean – killed.' We were now away from the primitive villagers, but their barbarity seemed to surround us.

'And they were buried in unconsecrated ground.'

The full force of the situation suddenly hit me. 'You mean the mounds –'

'Are their graves, yes. But their souls have been restive over the years, particularly if the house is inhabited.'

'You mean they'd like to drink *our* blood?' I asked him in horror.

But the priest shook his head. 'No – I think they only have one obsession: to gain admission to holy ground. To be cleansed and forgiven. To lie in peace.'

'So the vandals last night –'

'Were the Benoits, yes. But what can I do? I cannot let them into the graveyard.'

'Not even now?'

'No. If I exorcize them, hopefully their evil spirits will depart. It's something I have resisted doing until now. It's our last resort. And I suppose I am still afraid it might fail.'

'Are you going to tell my parents all this?' I asked.

'Of course. We are both priests, your father and I. We should have double strength. You must rely on me, my child.'

I was possessed by one thought. Don't bring my father into all this torment. Don't let my dear dad get mixed up in all this.

But a couple of hours later both he and the village priest were kneeling by the mounds, Bibles and crucifixes in hand, while my mother and I stood a few yards away. The afternoon was hot and the sweat ran into my eyes. The village priest intoned the prayers, Father provided the odd amen, and absolutely nothing happened. I could hear buzzing in the undergrowth, a dog howling somewhere in the village and, faintly, very faintly, the sound of a barge chugging up the lazy, sandy river.

After the priest left, Mum made light of the ritual. I suppose she was trying to cheer us up and not spoil the holiday. I now hoped the whole deadly business had been a dream, but as I went to bed I was afraid. My last thought was of my father's troubled face, refusing to be jollied out of his serious view by Mum. 'No,' he had told her. 'It really *isn't* just a superstitious ritual . . .'

★

I woke as the church clock struck two, with the familiar smell pervading the room.

Struggling to breathe, I got out of bed and ran to open the shutters. In the moonlight I saw the priest had returned and was standing silently on the mounds, holding aloft the cross from the altar of the church. As he said his incantations, the dry earth began to split open, the vile smell increased and the priest's voice faltered.

Then I heard my father hurrying down the stairs. I wanted to stop him going outside, but he was already opening the back door and striding across the scrubby, dew-laden grass towards the body of the priest, which now lay on the ground. Then I heard the gate click open.

The terrible couple were walking slowly but purposefully up the road, their ragged shapes just visible in the faint moonlight.

'Don't follow them,' said Dad.

'We've got to warn the village,' I cried.

But I needn't have panicked. The villagers were ready.

The dark crowd, armed with stakes, crosses and hammers, waited by the churchyard wall. The Benoits, arm in arm, walked towards them. I heard the dreadful sound of the dry husk of their voices as they pleaded – and pleaded again.

My parents took me away as the stakes found their mark.

A long silence followed Sarah's story. Then Jodie put her arms round her.

'Now,' said Tom. 'Let me tell you a story about a laboratory.'

6
A Deadly Experiment

For many years my friend Vic's father Don had been employed by STL, a specialist laboratory, which was under threat from government cutbacks. But surprisingly Don, a distinguished chemist, had recently resigned from the company.

His explanation seemed rational but out of character for such a dedicated scientist. 'I'm sorry, Vic. I can't take any more attacks and break-ins from these Animal Rights activists. I want to find a job somewhere which is safer. I have to think of you and your mother.'

The Animal Rights group considered STL were being cruel to the many mice, rats and monkeys they bred and studied. Don had always denied any cruelty and Vic had believed him implicitly. He was a good, kind man and would never hurt anything helpless. But now Don couldn't sleep and, in the early evenings, spent much of his time anxiously scanning the heavens. Was he having a nervous breakdown, wondered Vic.

On several occasions he had tried to tackle him, but his latest attempt met with a sharp rebuff.

'Dad.'

'Mm?' He was standing absently in the front room, looking out across the suburban street and up at the fading light in the autumn sky.

'What's up?'

'Up?' He looked startled and then recovered himself. 'Nothing. Nothing at all.'

'This is the fourth evening in a row I've found you here, looking up at the sky. Always at twilight. And you seem worried. *Something* must be going on.' There was no reply, but his father seemed to be gazing intently at a gaunt little tree in the opposite front garden. Vic watched his father's hands shake as he secured the latch on the window.

'You must make sure the windows are closed these early evenings.'

'But it's so hot —'

'There's an autumn chill. Definitely a chill. I don't want to find them open. I've already told your mother.'

'OK. What's so special about that tree?' asked Vic.

'What tree?'

'The one you were staring at just now.'

'Nothing. Nothing at all.'

Don moved away from the window quickly, pulling the curtains behind him, but not before Vic had seen what looked like a dark shape in amongst the top branches.

When he woke the next morning, the house was in commotion: his parents' voices were raised and his little sister was sobbing. What on earth could have happened, wondered Vic. Then he heard his mother's tread on the stairs. She knocked on the door but came in immediately, looking devastated.

'What's happened?' He was scared now, sitting bolt upright in bed. He had never seen her like this before.

'It's your dad's ex-colleague —'

'Professor Simmons?'

'He's been murdered. Your dad's gone down to the lab, but he said he'd be back as soon as he could.'

As it was a Saturday, Vic waited impatiently for his father to come home, but when he eventually arrived he looked stricken.

'Who was it?' Vic asked cautiously.

'They don't know. They're talking about muggers. But the police can't – oh, it doesn't matter.' He stopped short and it was as if a wall had come down between them.

'Dad –' Vic said desperately.

'Leave it!' His father replied sharply. 'Just leave it.'

Later, as Vic sat in his room, he heard the telephone ring and his father answer. There was some muttered conversation and then he heard the sound of a falling body. Vic rushed down to discover his father picking himself up, a look of horror on his face.

Vic was terrified. 'What's going on?' he demanded.

'He told me the same would happen to me,' he muttered.

'Who told you? And what will happen?'

Immediately his father clammed up. 'It's nothing. Something went wrong at the lab.'

'Another murder?'

'No. Nothing like that.'

'Then what?' demanded Vic.

His father paused, as if he was thinking quickly. 'An experiment went wrong. Someone got hurt, but not badly.' He was clearly pulling himself together now, shutting Vic out again. 'It was just a shock. I'm afraid that Professor Simmons' death – has made me – feel very shaken up. I'll go upstairs and lie down.'

Late in the afternoon, Vic decided to go to the lab. He

knew he wouldn't be allowed inside, but he had to think, make a plan, be near the place where such sinister events were happening. Above all, he *had* to devise some way to help his father.

The police had gone when he arrived at the long, low, one-storey building on the industrial estate at the edge of town. Looking at his watch, Vic saw that it was almost time for the staff to leave, so he hid in the space between the fence and the wall.

He waited for an hour until well after the staff had gone home. In fact the whole industrial estate emptied out at around six, so he thought it would be safe enough to have a look round the back of the building, even if he had no chance of getting in.

Vic climbed quickly over the fence and jumped down into the yard behind the lab. Then, after a long and panicky search, he was amazed to find a small window that would lever up sufficiently for him to squeeze through.

Vic had visited the building several times and, once inside, he soon found his way through to the main lab and headed towards the section where his father had worked. There was complete silence, except for the quiet humming of the central heating.

Fixed to a wall over one of the work stations was a cage with a heavy steel mesh on the front. It looked brand new; he definitely hadn't seen it on his previous visits. Vic thought there was a slight scratching sound inside, but before he could investigate he heard the sound of wheels on the drive outside. He froze. Could this be an intruder? An Animal Rights activist who might do him some harm? A minute or so later the sound of a key turning in a lock threw Vic into a state of total panic.

Where could he hide? There seemed nowhere in the

gleaming, methodically planned lab. The only possible place was a steel filing cabinet that stood slightly away from the wall and had cleaning materials behind it. Tucking himself into the gap with frantic speed, he managed to conceal himself, one foot all too near a can of cleaning fluid.

A few moments later a quiet, brisk, anonymously dressed man stepped into the room, and Vic instantly recognized him as STL's managing director, Simon Maxted. He was wheeling a trolley. Going over to the cage he detached it from the wall and held it up to the security light. Maxted stared inside for a good long time as if he was thinking deeply. Then he seemed to come to a decision. Slowly, carefully, he placed the cage on the trolley and stood listening. All Vic could hear was the dry scratching sound he had picked up earlier. He shuddered. What on earth could be inside that made such a sinister sound? A fanciful thought came into his head. Could the lab be developing some mutant species?

Maxted slowly, delicately, wheeled the trolley out of the room. Straining his ears, Vic heard the main door open, shut quietly and the key turn in the lock. After another minute or so, he could just make out the sound of a car engine. He listened until it died away. Then the silence around him deepened.

Squeezing his way cautiously out of the window and clambering over the fence without being seen, Vic walked slowly home. Why had Maxted been wheeling away a cage like that? He had only met him once or twice but Vic knew he was a much-respected local citizen: captain of the local cricket team, member of the Rotary club and general do-gooder, with a pleasant, open personality and known to be kind and helpful to his small staff. A good boss. But what was in the cage?

Vic knew he couldn't mention the incident to his father for fear of upsetting him further. He went to bed, intending to sleep on the problem, but in the early hours he suddenly found himself wide awake, fancying he had heard a sound, but muzzily wondering if he had been dreaming. Suddenly there was a low moan, and he sat up, shivering, his legs refusing to move. Forcing himself, Vic stumbled out of bed and ran downstairs.

His father was slumped in a chair with blood on his neck. Something was moving on the ceiling in the darkness. As Vic fumbled for the switch he heard the beating of wings, and when light finally flooded the room he saw the window was open – despite all Don's security precautions.

Rushing to his father's side, Vic immediately realized the wound in Don's neck was much deeper than he had thought. Ripping the cloth off the table, he tried to stanch the blood, and just as he was succeeding his mother appeared at the door.

'Get an ambulance,' Vic yelled at her.

'Can't let him get away with it,' his father muttered.

'Who?' asked Vic.

'Destroying the laboratory's reputation – just to breed the damn things. Crazy. He was told to stop. I told him to stop. But he's carrying on. He's trained the creatures to attack and to return to him. He must have been near by. Now he'll pick us off one by one.' He talked on, pleading with Vic to do something, eventually collapsing into delirium as the ambulance sped him away.

Vic went to look at the window in the front room, and examining it carefully noticed the catch had been forced from the outside. Sick with fear, he knew there was only one thing to do: he must return to the lab straightaway, giving himself no time to chicken out.

He squeezed in through the window again and crept quietly in the half-light towards the main laboratory. Then he froze.

Someone was in the kitchen, drinking coffee and writing feverishly on a lined pad. It was Maxted. Vic hesitated, staring nervously round the room. Then, without warning, something flew at him – huge, dark and furry. It hit him with such force that he fell against the wall. His head reeling, Vic stared up at it, realizing to his horror he was gazing at a giant bat. He heard the flapping of its dry wings, saw the mouse-like head, the bulbous eyes deep set, the teeth sharp as needles. Then, with unerring accuracy, the bat fastened its teeth in his neck.

Vic fell to the floor, thrashing wildly, tearing at the thing, but it clung on, its incisors deep in a fold of his neck and the bright-red blood spurting out of the wound. He rolled, but the bat still clung, and although he tried to claw it away, the creature was like a leech. Finally, just as he was weakening, a surge of fury swept over him, and with renewed strength he tore the bat away, the blood streaming down his fingers.

Desperately, he ran to the window and tried to lever up the security catch, but he couldn't free it and once again he heard the fluttering above him. He *had* to get the window open, but he still couldn't work out how to do it. He pushed, pulled – and it suddenly swung out. The bat dived, Vic ducked and fell, this time cracking his head on the steel filing cabinet. As the dark tunnel rushed towards him, he saw Maxted standing by the kitchen door, furiously angry, shouting. The bat hovered, and then dived once more.

Vic came to and looked at his watch. He had been unconscious for over five minutes. Shaking, he stumbled to his feet, went over to one of the work-benches and leaned against it, trying to recover. Then he caught sight of an outstretched body in the doorway. Simon Maxted lay in a pool of blood, his throat torn out.

Fearfully, Vic began to search the lab, but could find no trace of the giant bat. The window was still open, so he assumed that once the thing had gorged and become satiated, it had flown out into the night. What Maxted obviously hadn't realized was that the thing would not just be content to suck one victim dry.

Vic went over to the phone and called the police. Then he made sure all the windows of the lab were well fastened and all doors closed. When the squad arrived he was at the front of the building, carefully checking the sky.

When Vic's father had partially recovered, he told the police shakily what he knew.

'A giant fruit bat had never been bred in captivity before, but Maxted succeeded. He was a brilliant scientist, but he knew the other directors would never allow him to continue with such an experiment – it would have been completely against the laboratory's policy. We discovered what he was attempting and tried to dissuade him, but when he refused we were too weak to prevent him. When Professor Simmons and I saw the result – that enormous blood-sucking bat, and realized he was training it like a hawk – we threatened to report him, so he set the thing on Simmons and then on me.' He lay back in bed, staring out beyond the policemen at the foot of the bed. 'Nurse,' he called. 'Can you *close* that window?'

A few hours later, Don called Vic from the hospital, in considerable agitation.

'I think Terry should be investigated.'

'Who's Terry?' asked Vic in bewilderment.

'Maxted's son. He's also a scientist and I know they were very close. He was fascinated by his father's experiments and was working from a lab in his cottage just outside Weymouth. I think the police should get to him. Now.'

Vic rang the station at once and gave the investigating officer Terry Maxted's address, but when the local CID called, the cottage was deserted, and the equipment in the small laboratory hastily ripped out. Reports were coming in of something very large circling in the night sky.

'What's that?' hissed Jon.

Tom looked up to the arched ceiling of the crypt. Was that something fluttering?

'But do you think Maxted's son is still breeding them secretly somewhere?' asked Rob.

Tom shrugged. 'Vic doesn't know.'

There was a long, uneasy silence until Rob cleared his throat. 'We had a bad experience last year, didn't we, Jack?'

Jack shuddered. 'It was awful.'

'Shall I tell the story — or will you?'

'You tell it,' said Jack.

7
Family Thirst

Jack and I live near Newquay and we got a holiday job fixing up an old fishing trawler that was hauled up on the beach. She was called *Grey Eyes* and had been accidentally rammed in a storm. The family that owned the trawler, the Michaelsons, were quite happy for us to carry out the repairs, even though they were quite extensive. We were both delighted, because the job was worth a good deal of money and we had been promised payment at top rates.

When we talked to the locals they told us that the Michaelsons didn't use their boat for fishing, just to live on, and scoffingly dismissed them as 'water gypsies' and 'ageing hippies', but it didn't matter to us. They were our first clients and we wanted them to be really pleased with what we did.

While Jack and I carried out the work, the family rented an old beach hut in which they proposed to live. The Michaelsons moved their possessions overnight and never came out during the day, only emerging in the early evening, dressed in home-made clothes and certainly looking rather weird. Leslie and Arabella were the parents, somewhere in middle age, and Emelia was their teenage daughter. She was beautiful, and I know Jack was attracted to her – and she to him. They would walk up and down the beach in the twilight, talking and holding hands until I realized, with a twinge of envy, that my brother had fallen in love.

One morning, while the Michaelsons were in their hut with the door locked as usual, old Frank Lombard, a local fisherman and well-known Nosy Parker, came up for a gossip. He was full of some story the coastguards had told him.

'There's been more disappearances at sea on this part of the coastline than any other – that's what they're saying.'

'Been bad weather for a long time,' Jack reminded him, and I said, 'You sure of that?' Frank was a real old yarn-spinner and we didn't like him to get away with anything – which he did most of the time.

He shook his grizzled head and packed a pipe with blackened tobacco with obvious relish. 'Those ships were like the *Mary Celeste*,' he said, his eyes gleaming. 'Empty, drifting. God only knows where the crews went. Nothing to do with the weather.'

'I haven't seen anything in the papers,' said Jack suspiciously.

'That's because they're hushing it up.' Frank's eyes were full of morbid delight. 'Just in case folks get too frightened of their own shadows.'

'Since when have the papers hushed anything up?' I asked, but he ignored me. Frank didn't like interruptions.

'There's been a couple of disappearances recently – but there's going to be many more.'

'How do you work that out?' I asked.

'There's something out there.'

'A sea monster?' Jack almost laughed, only just managing to hold back his disbelief.

'Maybe. There's something preying on seafarers and that's the way I see it.' Eventually he ambled off, and we immediately dismissed the whole business. He was well known for exaggeration as well as being the great bore of Newquay, but though neither of us admitted it, this story did leave a lingering unease. I didn't like the idea of the crews just disappearing without trace. But, of course, it was only one of Frank's yarns.

'I'm going to take a look at the bilges,' said Jack. 'I think one of them's still going to leak – however much caulking we've done.'

He was away some time. Then he called me rather abruptly.

Crouched together in the hold, he showed me the metal cask he had found.

'Thought I'd take a look at what's inside,' he said. 'Let's go up into the light.'

We clambered back on deck and he poured some of the contents of the cask on to the planking. The liquid ran red.

'What is it?' I asked.

'Must be wine. I saw a lot of these casks in the Michaelsons' hut when I went to visit Emelia the other night.'

'That colour?' I sniffed, but it didn't smell of anything in particular. 'Maybe I should have a taste.'

'No.' Jack was immediately agitated.

'Why not?'

'It could be anything. Poison. Some chemical,' he suggested. 'Besides, if anything happened to you, I wouldn't be able to finish this job for ages.'

'Thanks a lot,' I said laughing. 'Seriously though, I wonder why they bothered to shift all those other casks into the hut. Do you think this red stuff's valuable?'

'Valuable to them obviously.' We both gazed at each

other, our curiosity rising, despite our determination to pay attention only to the job in hand.

'I'll tell you what.'

'Yes?' But Jack was already shaking his head. He knew what I was thinking.

'Let's go and take a look.'

'Spy on them? We can't do that. Emelia would be upset.' He looked shifty.

The old cliché was true, I thought bitterly. Love is blind.

Jack put the cask back in the bilges and we clambered down the ladder that was propped up against the trawler's bows. It was lunchtime and the beach was deserted. The sun was very hot for late spring, but I knew it was the rising anxiety that was really responsible for making us both sweat so heavily.

'Come on,' I said. 'Let's take a quick peek.'

Jack shrugged and followed grudgingly. But I knew his curiosity was slowly getting the better of him.

We crept up to the Michaelsons' ramshackle hut and furtively tried to peer through the grimy window. Unfortunately a large sheet of cardboard had been nailed in place and completely concealed the interior.

'Now what?' breathed Jack.

'Maybe the door's open.'

'You can't just walk in!'

'Why not?' Suddenly I was absolutely desperate to know what was inside. But the door was locked.

'We've got to *stop* this spying,' said Jack rather priggishly.

'On your girlfriend?' I goaded, annoyed and disappointed at not being able to satisfy what was now insatiable curiosity.

'I love her,' Jack said simply and directly and I knew he meant every word of it. Jack is far more passionate than I, and I could sense that Emelia was fast becoming an obsession.

'She's weird.' We'd withdrawn down the beach a little, but were still talking in whispers.

'She's beautiful. So shut up!'

'And I still say she's weird.'

'What do you want? A punch in the face?'

He was getting really worked up now, and as he is bigger than me I decided to back off.

'Hey – look at that!' I suddenly noticed part of the planking on the other side of the beach hut had rotted away, leaving a small hole. 'Bet we could see through there,' I said hopefully, trying to encourage him.

'Leave it.'

'Come on! We've got to check this out – whatever "this" is. And you know you'll feel better about Emelia then.'

He followed reluctantly as I tried to walk quietly over the pebbles, but they still made an incredibly loud scrunching sound.

As we crouched down I could see that an attempt had been made to block the hole, but the piece of tin they had used had fallen away.

'Blimey,' whispered Jack directly his eye was pressed to the planking. 'I don't get this.'

'What is it?' I demanded, in growing frustration.

'It *is* weird.' His voice trembled slightly.

'Let me see!' I could hardly bear the waiting now.

'I just don't believe it.' Jack was getting into a terrible state.

'*Please.*'

'OK. But don't make a noise – whatever you do.'

I squinted through the hole and with a creeping unease saw the three Michaelsons stretched out in hammocks, a cask below them and three empty glasses, stained red, on the table. They were all asleep, heavy and contented, their chests rising and falling in happy repose. I would have gasped out loud had Jack not suddenly grabbed my wrist.

We kept staring, taking it in turns to look, amazed at the sight. Then our amazement gave way to the first trickling chill of fear. There was something very unnatural going on here.

We moved slowly and cautiously away from hut. The beach looked as ordinary and innocent as ever, with the sun shining and the calm, glassy sea lapping gently at the pebbles. Everywhere there was normality – except in the battered beach hut with its equally battered nameplate which read: *DUNROAMIN*.

'What had they been drinking?' I asked Jack, as we walked slowly down the beach towards the sea.

'Wine. What else? They're a bunch of alcoholics. I'd like to save her. Take Emelia away from them.' But he sounded more anxious than condemning, as if he was trying to shut something out of his mind.

'What are we going to do then?'

'*I* don't know. Let me think.'

But was it *really* wine, I asked myself, turning back and gazing at the hut. Then I looked into my brother's eyes. Was he thinking what I was?

We returned to working on *Grey Eyes*, and the long, lazy afternoon stretched around us without a breath of wind, as we hammered and caulked the chine-built sides of the trawler that we were now sure hadn't been used for fishing in years. She didn't even smell of fish. Then I noticed something coming in with the tide. The object nudged against the bank of pebbles and resembled an old tarpaulin.

'Jack –'

We both trudged slowly round to the pebble bank, but it wasn't a tarpaulin after all. It was the corpse of a middle-aged man in a blue sweater and jeans, floating on his front. He wore long seaman's boots.

'He looks kind of deflated, doesn't he?' said Jack, once again horribly voicing my own thoughts.

Then we heard a choking cough behind us and wheeled round to see Frank, puffing on his pipe, gloomy pleasure written all over his wrinkled face. 'Another one.'

I stared at him blankly. 'What do you mean?'

'That's what they all look like when they're washed up.'

'You mean – the men on the boats?' Jack asked slowly. 'You said they went missing.'

'Didn't want to alarm you – not two young kids like yourselves. Besides, the police told us to keep mum while they were investigating, like.' Frank was really enjoying himself now. 'Sucked dry,' he muttered. 'Like they all were.'

'What are we going to do with the body?'

'Leave it to us.' There was a new authority to his voice which took me by surprise.

'Who's us?' I asked.

'The fishermen,' he said. 'We'll deal with the body. But if only we knew the cause . . .'

It was then that I decided to tell Frank what we had seen in the beach hut.

Jack, however, was frowning. 'Aren't we jumping to conclusions?' he asked. 'In my opinion the Michaelsons have got a drink problem. They need help.'

'They've got a problem all right,' said Frank, 'but it's the innocent seafarers who need the help.'

There was a long and brooding silence during which I saw Jack's eyes fill with angry tears.

'We'll drag the corpse out and shove it under that dinghy.' Frank was completely in charge now.

'Aren't you going to call the police?' I asked.

'In due course.'

'But –'

'You carry on repairing that trawler. I don't want the Michaelsons alerted.' He turned to gaze at the hut with a vengeful eye.

'When *will* the police come?' asked Jack insistently.

'When we're finished. But you work, you hear. Come sundown you'll go home.' His voice was harsh and I realized that he saw himself and his comrades as vigilantes.

'I can't,' said Jack. Both he and I knew that the fishermen were going to do something appalling to the Michaelsons.

'You'll go home,' said Frank fiercely. 'You'll do what I say. Do you hear?'

We nodded, knowing that we wouldn't obey him. After we had lugged the corpse ashore and laid it under the upturned dinghy, he walked purposefully away to some fishermen further down the beach, grouped around an old winch.

'I've got to warn her,' said Jack frantically. 'I've got to save her.'

'You can't.'

'I must!'

'You can't help the Michaelsons escape.' I was furious at his tunnel vision. 'You know what they are, don't you?'

'It could be a mistake,' he muttered.

'How?' I asked bluntly.

We both gazed up and down the beach to see that two lines of fishermen were mending nets that stretched right down to the sea, blocking all access.

★

An hour later, Frank walked back to us.

'I've changed my mind,' he said.

'Have you?' I asked flatly.

'You'll stay.'

'Stay?' protested Jack. 'You said –'

'You'll stay until we've finished with them.' I could see the hatred in his eyes, and suddenly I was as afraid of him as I was of the Michaelsons. But I knew Jack felt differently. I could feel the intensity of the anger surging within him.

We continued apprehensively working on *Grey Eyes*. Then, as darkness fell, Jack said to me, his eyes full of a terrible desperation, 'I've *got* to warn her.'

There was a sudden blaze of light at each end of the beach and I saw the fishermen had lit a couple of braziers, which were flaring up like beacons.

'You mustn't go near the hut.'

'I have to.'

I grabbed him and we struggled, but Jack is much stronger than me. In the end he hit me hard and I fell back on to the pebbles. From my prone position I watched my brother dash over the nets and stride towards the hut, but just as he drew near, the door opened and Emelia stood there, beautiful in the moonlight.

'You've got to get away,' said Jack desperately.

'Why?' She looked genuinely puzzled.

'You – we – they're going to get you,' he stuttered.

'They?'

'Look,' I said, getting up and running towards them. 'Just look.'

The two lines of fishermen were slowly advancing on the beach hut and in their hands were flaming torches. Their eyes were vengeful in the fiery light and their step had a deadly, unyielding purpose.

Emelia looked terrified as the fishermen approached.

Then her parents quietly joined her at the door. Taking one look at what was happening, Mr Michaelson said to Jack, 'Get her away. Please get her away.'

Jack grabbed Emelia's hand and they began to run. I yelled out, 'She'll kill you.' But he wasn't listening, and I saw they were heading for the town. Standing there on my own, I had this terrible vision of Jack lying somewhere, his body limp, drained of blood.

But two young fishermen had set off at a tremendous pace. They dragged them both back, Jack in a half-nelson and Emelia, her head held high, the terror in her eyes dreadful to witness. I knew that she realized she was going to be executed.

Her parents had already been escorted on to *Grey Eyes* and the fishermen stood in a half-circle, their flaming torches held aloft as Emelia was taken on board.

The Michaelsons were locked in the wheelhouse and I could see their faces at the glass. There was a calm dignity to them, and Emelia had her eyes fixed on my brother.

Frank tossed his torch on board, followed by the others, while the two young fishermen held my brother down as he kicked and struggled and yelled. He called her name over and over again as the flames took a steady hold and the trawler was a roaring roasting death-ship.

As Emelia's face was obscured by black smoke, my brother wept uncontrollably.

Jack looked away as Rob finished the story. The others stared restlessly at each other.

Unable to bear the silence any longer, Mary glanced round the cold desolation of the moonlit crypt and said, 'Blood was something that my friend Sharon was quite willing to give. Until she realized what it was needed for.'

8
The Undertaker's Parlour

Sharon couldn't get a job. She wasn't that bright and she interviewed badly. Both her parents were out of work and she was determined to make a contribution to the family budget. Although not academically clever, she cared deeply for others and was a popular girl who everyone wanted to help and support.

Her job-hunting did not start well. She scanned the notice-boards at the Job Centre, but either there was nothing she was qualified to do, or when she went for the interview she became a stuttering wreck. Then one day she saw a small card at the bottom of the board:

WANTED
QUIET SYMPATHETIC PERSON AS
RECEPTIONIST FOR UNDERTAKER
APPLY – B.T. JENNINGS

I could do that, she thought. Providing it didn't mean any typing or adding up. I'm good at being sympathetic to people. What's more, I really like people, and surely that would be a good qualification for the job.

Feeling quite hopeful, Sharon went to the woman behind the counter in the Job Centre – a Mrs Burdock whom she knew quite well – and asked her what she thought about B.T. Jennings.

'He's *always* advertising,' Mrs Burdock replied.

'Always?'

'Well – more often than not.'

'But why?'

'He can't keep his staff. The receptionists leave regularly, but *we've* never been given a reason.'

'Perhaps they can't get on with him,' suggested Sharon.

Mrs Burdock smiled. 'Maybe you're right.' She was very fond of Sharon – even if she was difficult to place. 'You've got such a sweet nature. I'm sure you'll suit Mr Jennings well.'

Mr Jennings wasn't like an undertaker, or at least, not what Sharon thought an undertaker should be like. She had imagined a long, thin, cadaverous man with a soft voice, his head slightly bowed, a fawning smile on his face. But instead Mr Jennings was fat and bouncy, jovial and smiley. 'Call me Brian,' he said straightaway. Sharon was shocked, and determined to call him Mr Jennings, but he wouldn't let her. After they had talked for a while he said, 'Well, Miss Hewitt, I'm sure you and I are going to get on very well. When can you start?'

'Well – soon.'

'Tomorrow?'

'Er –'

'And may I call you Sharon?'

She supposed he might.

Sharon began the job as receptionist at the undertaker's the following day and was soon thoroughly enjoying every moment. Of course, it was sad, but she was delighted to bring comfort to the many bereaved people who called and pass them on to Mr Jennings – Brian, as he still kept insisting she must call him – or his young and attractive assistant Sam. He couldn't have been much older than she and was 'learning the ropes' as Brian put it, and 'getting on jolly well'. And as far as Sharon was concerned she was 'super' and 'a real treasure'.

Best of all, she didn't have to go anywhere near the corpses, which were kept in a place Brian called 'behind the scenes'. All she had to do was to stay on reception, amongst the plastic lilies and display headstones, with her discreet forms and smiling sympathy.

Then, one morning, a young girl arrived and sat down at Sharon's desk abruptly. 'Can I help you?' Sharon said gently.

'Mr Jennings out?' the girl asked, glancing around furtively.

'Er – yes.'

'Sam out?' Her eyes darted into every part of the room.

'Both at a funeral. Have you been bereaved?' asked Sharon sympathetically.

'Not exactly.'

'Then how can I help you?' She was bewildered now, uneasily wondering if her visitor was mad.

'I've come to warn you.'

'What?' Now she was convinced the young girl was disturbed.

'Warn you to leave. Now! Just walk out.'

Sharon drew herself up stiffly, mustering all her self-confidence. She had meant to be diplomatic, but instead she was angry and indignant. She loved her job and didn't want it cheapened like this. 'How dare you suggest such a thing! Who are you?'

'Let me explain.' The girl looked around again, a

little pulse twitching in her cheek. 'That Mr Jennings –'

'Yes?'

'Brian. He's – not what he seems.'

'I don't understand.' Sharon was freezingly polite.

'He's dangerous. Very dangerous.'

This must be some kind of absurd joke, Sharon thought. Well, she wasn't putting up with it.

'I knew no one would believe us – but that's why we left.' The girl was close to tears.

'*We?*'

'The receptionists. But that's not everything. He's asked us – all of us – if – if –' The girl faltered, unable to continue.

'I don't understand.' Sharon stared at her blankly. 'This is a joke in very poor taste and I'd be obliged if you left.'

'That was the problem – no one would believe us. Mr Jennings is a well-respected member of the community.'

'Naturally.' Sharon stood up, trying to seem as threatening as possible.

'Everyone thought we fancied him. That we were making up awful stories.'

'You are! Now get out, or I'll call the police.'

'We all swore that we'd warn other receptionists. We formed an association – and we meet regularly. We're determined to bring Mr Jennings to justice. You can help – get some evidence. Let me try to explain what he's up to.'

Sharon stood up and opened the door, determined to assert herself. I suppose she reckons I'm thick, she thought. Thick enough to believe her rotten joke.

'I'm only trying to –' the girl started to say.

'Go!'

The girl went.

★

'Oh, Sharon —'

She was still shaken, and took a while to reply. 'Yes, Mr — er — Brian?'

'Can you step into my office?'

'Of course.' She followed Mr Jennings into his office — a large, expensive room with a huge desk, and filled with pictures of cemeteries and crematoria.

'How are you enjoying it here?' Mr Jennings leaned back in his swivel chair, plump and affable.

'Very much.'

'I was wondering if you'd like a rise?'

'But I've only been here a few days,' said Sharon in surprise.

'Nevertheless — you must realize I'm most pleased with you.'

'Thank you.'

'I'd like to offer you another pound an hour — as well as my special bonus.'

'Bonus?'

'Yes — to help with my private blood bank.'

'Your what?' She gazed at him in bewilderment.

'I assemble blood types. For hospital use, of course. It's a charity I run. Registration number 16143262B.'

'I see. I'd get a bonus for this, would I?'

'A substantial one.'

'And what would I have to do?'

'I'd just like you to give some of your blood.' He smiled beguilingly. 'You've no idea how short the National Health Service is at the moment.'

'You're qualified? I mean, forgive me, but —' Sharon was flustered now, anxious not to appear impertinent.

'Of course. You *must* ask these questions. You wouldn't be a responsible person if you didn't — and neither would I. But naturally enough, I'm qualified. I took a special course and am able to receive and store

68

the blood of my donors. In fact I'm an SBDSC. A Special Blood Donor Supply Consultant. Registered, of course, by the MOH.'

'And that is?' She flushed slightly.

He raised his eyebrows gently. 'Ministry of Health.'

'Of course.' Why was she always so stupid?

'And then there's the bonus. Two hundred pounds.'

'Goodness!' That's a lot of money, thought Sharon. I thought blood donation was voluntary. 'How much blood would you like me to give, Brian?' she asked hesitantly.

'A couple of pints.'

'Very well.' There – she had made up her mind. Normally this took her some time, but it was good to be decisive for once.

'Thank you. The patients at the Royal Infirmary are going to benefit. Shall we step through?'

'Now?'

'No time like the present, Sharon.'

'Of course, Brian.'

He unlocked the door at the back and she followed him through to a small room that was stacked with bottles of red liquid.

'I'll just get a syringe.'

'You *have* got a lot of donors, Brian.'

'People are generous, Sharon,' he said, lifting down an empty bottle. 'People are very generous.'

Suddenly the outer office door opened and Sam stood on the threshold. Behind him were half a dozen women, one of whom Sharon instantly recognized. She frowned. How dare they intrude. Didn't they know when a joke was well and truly over? And why was Sam involved in all this?

Brian frowned. 'A deputation?'

'Yes,' replied Sam. 'I think we've caught you in the act at last, Mr Jennings.'

'Now look here —' began Brian, but when Sharon glanced at him she could see that his normally ruddy complexion was now pale and sweaty and his jovial tone had become halting.

'No,' said Sam. '*You* look here! Right?'

'Right,' nodded the six ex-receptionists. Their eyes were on Mr Jennings — eyes that were full of hatred and triumph.

'I've got photographs, Mr Jennings,' said Sam. 'Photographs of you. I'm afraid the hospital doesn't benefit, does it? But you do. Now — are you coming down to the police station, or shall I make a citizen's arrest?'

'I shall have to call my solicitor.' Brian made a stab at composure.

'You're welcome.'

'He'll soon help me clear all this up.'

'I'll stay here and mind the shop,' said Sam to the receptionists. 'If you'll escort Mr Jennings down to the station.'

Left on their own together, Sam grinned at Sharon conspiratorially.

'Will he really be arrested?' she asked. Her mind was in utter confusion and she couldn't get to the explanation, although dawning horror was slowly sweeping over her.

'You bet. I've got too much evidence against him — been gathering it ever since I discovered what he was up to about a year ago. He'll go down for a long time.'

'I'm very grateful to you,' said Sharon. 'And I'm sure all the other receptionists are.'

'It was terrible, watching them all succumbing to his charm.' Sam was very sympathetic.

'Well, I did the same and I suppose I'm out of a job now. But what exactly . . .'

'The business won't fold,' replied Sam. 'If I can work out all the legal complications I'll be able to take it over.'

'But when it all gets out,' said Sharon, the appalling truth dawning on her at last. 'I mean – relatives aren't exactly going to want to deposit their loved ones with us, are they?'

'I'll change the name,' he said. 'Don't worry about it.' Sam locked the door. 'We've got plenty of spare coffins.'

'*What?*'

'I've often found them useful when I've been out on the streets at night and brought my girls back here. They always thought it was a really good joke to come back to an undertaker's for a kiss and cuddle. The joke went a bit sour for them, but not for me. I could dump the bodies in Leysdown Lake before dawn. Anyone who saw the hearse loaded with a coffin probably thought I was heading for the hospital mortuary.'

'I don't know what you mean.' Sharon's mind was now going round in circles. Obviously this must be another joke.

'Brian ran his racket – and I run mine. But I'm the genuine article. Brian liked to drink it out of a bottle. But I like it straight from the neck.' He laughed.

'I simply don't get you,' said Sharon. But this time she was lying . . .

Jon's feet were icy cold. He wished they could light a fire. 'Has anyone else got a story?'

Abby spoke first. 'Well, there was the time we got lost in the Forest of Dean . . .'

9
The Prowler

We almost didn't get to stay with my old aunt. The night we were due to go, she phoned and told my cousin Fiona and me that we weren't to come after all. Fortunately, my parents were out.

'You see, my dear – I'd be afraid for you.'

'Afraid?'

'There have been two awful – killings up here.' Aunt Jane wasn't the superstitious or the panicky type. Her husband had died years ago and she was a strong, independent woman who loved the forest. Uncle Alfred used to be in the Forestry Commission, and she had a tied cottage that was very isolated. Nobody could persuade her to move, despite the long journeys she had to make down lonely paths to the nearest village. I had been on visits with my parents, but never without them, and I was really looking forward to Fiona and I being on our own together. We were great friends and thoroughly enjoyed each other's company.

'Murders?' I asked ghoulishly.

'No, dear. Killings.'

'Any suspects?'

'The police think it's an animal – perhaps even an animal that has escaped from a zoo and gone wild. It's already attacked two locals.'

Eventually, however, after a great deal of persuasion, I won her round by saying that we wouldn't roam about in the forest at all, but would call a taxi to take us into the town. 'But are *you* still going out alone?' I asked protectively.

'Well –'

'You see. Why don't *you* call a taxi?'

'I like to walk. To be independent.' An impatient note came into Aunt Jane's voice. 'And no animal gone wild is going to scare me off,' she added fiercely. 'They say I ought to have a dog to protect me but –' her voice softened – 'I've adopted a cat. Lovely, sleek, gracious animal. She's real company for me.'

'What's its name?' I asked curiously. Aunt Jane had never liked cats when Uncle Alfred had been alive. 'Nasty independent things,' she had always said. 'Got minds of their own.'

'*Her* name, dear. Midnight.'

'Where did you find her?'

'Roaming in the forest. I advertised, but no one claimed her – so she's mine!' She paused. 'As you may remember, I've never liked cats much, but this one – she seems to love the cottage. Always hiding upstairs, licking her lips.' She laughed. 'Maybe I've just got into being a lonely old woman, but sometimes, when I see Midnight running home, I rather enjoy the feeling that I'm protecting *her*.'

'Well, *she* certainly won't be able to protect you from a wild animal, will she?'

'I can look after myself.' Aunt Jane sounded cross, so I changed the subject quickly.

We arrived on a rather cold autumn day and found the trees had turned to rustling gold. It was so beautiful and as deep and as dark as any fairy-tale forest might be.

Deep and dark and mysterious – just like Midnight. She was really impressive, beautifully brushed and well cared for by Aunt Jane.

'Now, you're not going wandering out there,' she said.

We knew we were, but we certainly weren't going to tell her.

'We'll stay in sight of the cottage,' I said reassuringly.

She looked doubtful. 'Well, mind you do. And don't go talking to that Barnes.'

'Who?'

'Silas Barnes. He works for the forestry. Only got a tiny place, him and his wife and children. Barnes would like to get me out. Have me evicted.'

'How do you make that out, Aunt Jane?' asked Fiona.

Aunt Jane gave her a particularly nasty look. 'You saying I'm imagining things, young woman?'

'Of course not!'

'I can see it in his eyes. His greedy eyes. He wants me out and him in.'

It's a pity that we disobeyed our aunt and didn't stay near the cottage, because after about ten minutes of walking Fiona and I realized we were lost. The trees seemed to have grown even more thickly together, the light was shut out and we found ourselves wandering through the gloom of a dense, dark canopy of leaves. The forest was silent – a silence only occasionally broken by a soft scrabbling sound which came and went, as if something was crouched, watching us, waiting to spring. Then a man emerged abruptly from the trees.

He was tall and extremely thin, with a rough beard that partly concealed a long, livid scar which made him look particularly menacing.

'You lost?' he asked roughly.

'No,' I said.

'Yes,' replied Fiona.

'Make up your minds then.' He grinned and the scar puckered. 'You must be Mrs Atkins' nieces.'

'How do you know?' I said coldly.

'News travels fast in the forest.'

'We're just going for a walk.'

'But we don't know how to get back,' Fiona chipped in, looking rather scared. 'Can you show us?' she asked nervously.

'I wouldn't go back to the cottage if I were you,' he said gently.

'*What?*' I gasped.

'I'd go home.' The man wasn't grinning now and his eyes were full of concern.

'I'd like to point out,' I said pompously, 'that we're visiting our own aunt.'

'That's why I'd go home. Why not come back to my place and I'll call a taxi. There's a good track down to the village.'

'How dare you!' I said, outraged that he should order us around like that.

But Fiona was interested. 'What's all this about?'

'You know who this man is, don't you?' I interrupted. 'He's Silas Barnes – the man who's trying to get Aunt Jane evicted.'

'I'm doing no such thing,' he said indignantly.

'*She* thinks you are.'

'That's because she's old and insecure.' Barnes hesitated and then added, stumbling over his words, 'She's not as – as clear-thinking as she used to be.'

'Of course she is,' I snapped.

'I'm afraid she's not,' he persisted. 'She's getting absent-minded – and that's dangerous.'

'She doesn't want to go into a home.'

'No. But the council have offered her a flat in a sheltered-housing scheme. With a warden. She'd be safe there.'

'She wouldn't like that.' I was insistent. 'Aunt Jane wants to keep her independence, and you know how she loves the forest.'

'But she'd be safe,' he repeated. 'Don't forget – there's this thing wandering about. Attacking people. You two shouldn't be around on your own like this. Didn't she warn you? We don't know what kind of creature this is – but it likes blood. What's more, it needs the stuff. I've searched this part of the forest very thoroughly, but it's clearly got itself some kind of hiding-place.'

'Yes,' said Fiona. 'She warned us not to leave the cottage, but we thought it would be all right to go on just a little.'

'Ah.' He smiled at her again, a broader smile this time and I caught a glimpse of his ragged teeth. They seemed to be all little sharp points. 'Come on – I'll take you back to your aunt's. Then we can collect your bags and get a taxi from there.' He suddenly shivered and listened. Then he said urgently, 'You will get your parents to talk to her, won't you?' Silas Barnes looked directly at me now. 'She's taking on too much. Adopting that damned stray.'

'Midnight? She's lovely,' I returned. 'Aunt Jane is lonely. Needed a pet.'

'That thing? A pet? I've been wondering –' he muttered, and then ended abruptly. 'Come on then. I haven't got much time, but I'll see you back.'

'There's no need,' I insisted.

'Oh, but, Abby –' began Fiona anxiously.

'Shut up!'

Barnes gave me a reproving look and as he opened his mouth to admonish me, I saw those sharp little teeth once again. Wasn't one of them a little longer, sharper than the others, or was it my imagination?

'No,' I snapped. 'Tell us the way and we'll go alone.'

Reluctantly he gave some clear directions. We walked hurriedly away, but when I turned round I could see that he was standing under one of the tallest of the trees, watching us. As we almost ran down the path I could feel the damp chill of the forest and could smell rotting leaves, moss and fir-cones. I had the uncomfortable feeling that the forest was breathing on us – and its breath was moist and fetid.

The shadows of the trees lengthened and darkened. Could we have come so far? Were we following Barnes's directions properly, or had we got lost again? We'd trusted him not to get us lost a second time.

Fiona didn't exactly try to raise my confidence. Hers had vanished long ago.

'Didn't he say turn right here?'

'No, left,' I replied angrily.

'You sure?'

'Of course I'm sure.'

'You never did have much sense of direction.'

'And you don't know anything about the forest,' I retorted.

'Do you?' Then Fiona paused. 'What was that?'

'I didn't hear anything.'

'Sort of soft, scuttling, scratching sound.'

'It's nothing – the forest's full of noises like that,' I said scornfully.

'It's stopped.'

'There you are then.' I was still angry, but secretly I was also beginning to feel afraid. 'Come on. It's getting dark.'

'Wait,' Fiona insisted. 'It's as if – it's as if something's watching us.'

I stared at her. The smell – the breath of the forest – seemed to intensify as a little dagger of breeze stirred the leaves.

'Suppose it's Barnes? Maybe he's following us,' I said.

'Who?' asked Fiona stupidly. I looked at her witheringly. How could I have imagined that we actually got along. She was thick, stupid – moronic.

'Silas Barnes.'

'Oh, him –'

'Yes, him. Suppose he's the murderer.'

'I thought he was rather nice.' I saw that she was staring at a patch of brambles. They were very thick and the berries looked almost obscenely ripe, swollen, purple; almost ready to burst.

'I didn't. Did you see his teeth?'

'What about his teeth? Stop talking rubbish.'

I could have slapped her for being so unobservant. What was more, she was whispering for some obtuse reason.

'What's the matter?' I snapped, annoyed to find that I was whispering too.

'He *is* following us. I can see him through the trees.'

A wave of fear and anger swept over me. 'Come *on*, Fiona,' I said urgently. 'What on earth are you staring at *now*?'

'See those eyes.'

'What eyes?'

'There in the brambles.'

Then I saw them. Huge. Yellow. Vicious-looking. Almost mocking us. The fear spread inside me and made me unable to move.

'What is it?'

'A cat,' she said.

Midnight sprang out at us spitting, her huge, black, sleek body arched.

'Stay where you are.' Fiona rapidly took charge of the situation. 'Don't move.'

I knew I couldn't.

Then, with a bound, she was running past us, her yellow eyes still mocking. Midnight disappeared down the path into the darkness.

'That's the way,' I said. 'I recognize that fallen log, don't you?' All my animosity and impatience with Fiona were lost as hope flooded through me. 'We're not that far from the cottage.'

Fiona didn't seem exactly overjoyed.

When we arrived back and opened the front door everything at first seemed very normal. Aunt Jane was sitting in her chair and Midnight was curled up on her lap. But then I saw that the cat was still licking the blood from her paws.

'I don't think Mr Barnes will be bothering me again,' said Aunt Jane.

'I'm going back up to the hostel.' Jane stood up and there was a relieved murmur of agreement.

'But I haven't told mine yet,' said Colin. 'There was this doll's house that my friend Derek told me about. I must tell you.'

10
The Doll's House

'I'm stuck with it now. Can't sell it. That wouldn't be right.'

Uncle Ernie often told Derek that he couldn't get rid of the antique doll's house. He said it came from somewhere in eastern Europe and was 'quite a collector's item'. But Derek was surprised by the sudden loathing in his eyes when he looked at the dusty, shuttered windows.

Derek's Uncle Ernie died last year and he left one extraordinary clause in his will: that the toy shop he had owned for so many years should not be sold and must remain closed and undisturbed for the remainder of Derek's life – a perverse instruction, as the premises were on a prime site in a South London suburb. While his family consulted with solicitors as to how to break the will and sell the shop, Derek's curiosity grew into an obsession. He just couldn't understand why his uncle had come to such a decision.

They had always been close and Ernie would tell Derek the most wonderful stories of the toys he had imported from all over the world. He was more of a collector of antiques than a trader and his clients were almost always other collectors.

Derek always received the same reply whenever he asked questions about the doll's house, but he often caught Uncle Ernie looking at it with hatred. As he grew older and more unwell, his uncle seemed to become increasingly anxious. Then, one afternoon, he gave Derek a key.

'What's this for?' Derek had asked.

'The shop. I don't want it sold when I'm dead – it must gather dust and stay as it is. I just want to ensure that nothing happens – no vandals break in or anything gets damaged. I'm giving you the key as a sacred trust, Derek. The only other one will be lodged with my solicitors. Give it to your parents if you think something is wrong – and only then. Will you do that for me?'

Derek nodded, puzzled by his uncle's vehemence.

'And promise that you won't come in here out of curiosity. There are some toys that I don't want sold – just out of sentiment – and there's one that should never see the light of day again.'

Derek crossed his fingers behind his back as he nodded this time, for he knew that he couldn't make that promise. The collection was precious, and he couldn't be locked out of it for ever.

A few months later, Uncle Ernie died and Derek was grief-stricken, but it wasn't for a further six months that he was tempted to go and unlock the shop, mostly out of respect for his uncle's wishes, but partly because he was afraid. Afraid of what, he often wondered. Was it just that he felt his uncle would be angry?

It was an early winter morning with a hard, bright sun when Derek finally decided to go inside. He hesitated for a long time and then quickly turned the key in the lock. All was still once he had closed the squeakingly stiff door behind him and the dust had settled.

The stillness was suffocating, and a rocking-horse's eyes looked at Derek, seemingly in mute appeal. So did the stuffed animals, the clockwork trains and old Meccano models; all looked lost and desolate, covered in cobwebs. He shuddered as the spiders scuttled, disturbed for the first time in months.

Then he became aware of another sound – a soft squeaking that could have been mice. He wasn't afraid of them; it was only the spiders that made him panic.

Then Derek realized that the squeaking was coming from the doll's house. There must be a mouse inside, probably destroying the valuable interior, but when he tried to lift the cobwebby roof it wouldn't move. As he wrestled with it, he dimly heard his uncle's words in his mind: 'There are some toys that I don't want sold – just out of sentiment – and there's one that should never see the light of day again.'

After a while he saw that a keyhole had been delicately cut out of one side of the doll's house wall. Derek fiddled with it for a while and then idly pushed the shop door key into the hole – and found it fitted exactly. Wary of any spiders, he turned it and pulled up the roof to reveal the top storey, noticing the squeaking had stopped. But there was no sign of any mice at all. Instead, a miniature female doll was lying on a bed and the long, thin figure of a gaunt-looking male doll was leaning over her with a minute cup in his hand. There was a gash in her throat from which a steady stream of blood was flowing into the cup.

Derek stared down in horrified amazement and then examined the other bedrooms, where he saw more torn plastic throats. It must be a macabre mechanical toy of some kind, but despite the fact that it was evil-looking, whoever had made the house must have been a considerable craftsman.

He examined the roof for a while and then saw a label written in German. Taking out his diary and pencil, Derek scribbled down the alien words.

Locking the shop carefully behind him, he hurried down to the local library and asked Mrs Cole, the librarian, to help him translate. She was always helpful and rarely asked the boring questions that most adults asked. Using a German dictionary she rapidly translated the words. They read: *This doll's house belongs to the Munlarst children. It was made for us by our beloved father, but he is now so blind that he cannot see. When he is dead, he wishes the house to accompany him.*

'Accompany him?' repeated Derek. 'Why would he wish that?'

'Perhaps he was a craftsman,' Mrs Cole explained. 'In the old days, the *very* old days, if a master craftsman died, the best example of his work would be buried with him.'

Derek was intrigued. 'But the doll's house couldn't have been in the coffin, could it? Right now it's in my uncle's old shop.'

'Wait a minute,' said Mrs Cole, leaning on her information desk and trying to remember something. 'Munlarst.'

'Yes?' said Derek encouragingly.

'Munlarst. Now where have I heard that name before?' She continued to ponder while he grew more and more impatient. Finally she exclaimed, 'Oh yes!'

'Well?'

'They were monsters.'

'Monsters? The Munlarsts?' He was amazed. What *could* she mean.

'Well, not exactly monsters.'

Derek was in an agony of frustration.

'It's all coming back now. I remember reading it in *Real-life Vampire Legends* – years ago.'

'Vampires?' interrupted Derek.

She frowned. 'Not quite so loud, dear.'

'Vampires?' he whispered.

'Now I remember the reference. Stefan and Eva Munlarst were reputed to be not only real-life vampires in eighteenth-century Romania, but also sorcerers. Stefan had an official trade as a cabinet-maker, but then he suddenly went blind; it was rumoured he had been cursed by a rival, so he couldn't see his victims and was unable to satisfy his thirst. Terrible old rubbish.' She laughed heartily – a little too heartily for Derek.

'Sorcerers?' He felt ill. The gash in the doll's tiny throat. Could it have been *real* blood? And as for the blind vampire . . .

'Now don't go filling your head with –' Mrs Cole began, but with muttered thanks Derek had gone before she could finish.

However scared he was he knew he had to go back to the shop while the light was at its best. Derek looked at his watch. Just after midday. If he made the mistake of waiting till the afternoon, it would be too dark to see properly.

He hurried back down the High Street, unlocked the door of the shop again and hesitated on the threshold, his nerves screaming. Then, somehow, Derek forced himself to walk in.

He slowly opened the roof of the doll's house and received an incredible shock. The man doll had disappeared, leaving the girl doll on the bed with those terrible markings on her neck. He tried to pull himself together, tried to remember that this was a toy. No more, no less. A macabre toy – a toy that manufactured artificial blood?

Who am I kidding, wondered Derek. Manufactured?

Derek slid away the front of the house to reveal the other floors. The first contained elegant rooms, corridors and hallways, which were beautifully furnished but contained no dolls – or dolls' blood. But when he began to investigate the cellar he saw something move, hide, move again and then scuttle on to the floor of the shop towards a pile of packing cases at the very back. Whatever it was, it definitely wasn't a mouse, although it seemed to squeak. Or was he hearing words – words that tumbled over each other in venomous fury. Derek's heart began to pound and the fear surged inside him, making him gasp with pain.

His gaze swept the cellar of the doll's house and he saw that most of the space was packed with row upon row of tiny coffins. About half of them were open – and inside one was a female doll with a great gash at her neck.

Derek drew back, knowing that he couldn't take much more of this. No wonder his uncle had been so afraid. Yet he had kept the doll's house. Why? Was it because he hadn't dared give it away? Uncle Ernie had been a good man and Derek knew he would never offload such a dreadful responsibility on to others.

Reluctantly and apprehensively, he walked down to the back of the shop, following the direction of the squeaking sound, and clambered up on top of the old packing-cases to find a long, wooden box where the noise seemed to have stopped. Not only was he terrified of what he might discover inside, but he was just as afraid of the even thicker cobwebs and the wildly scuttling spiders, some of which were enormously dark and hairy.

Derek brushed aside the debris, wiping clear the shipping label that read: MODEL SOLDIERS FROM ROMANIA. FRAGILE. THIS WAY UP. He tried to push and pull at the lid of the box, but soon found that it was sealed. Somehow he would have to break it open. There was a small hole on the top, but he could hardly get his finger into it and there was no leverage at all.

After finding a hammer and chisel, he spent half an hour banging and prising up the lid, which finally split open in a rending and tearing of dusty wood. Nothing could have prepared Derek for what he saw as he gazed, stupefied, into the wooden box.

Inside was the full-length figure of a rosy-cheeked gentleman in foreign-looking clothes, who was soundly and peacefully asleep, his chest rising and falling rhythmically. At his side was a small cup of red blood. Squeaking at Derek angrily, a tiny creature crept from behind the figure and then ran back down the packing cases to the doll's house – but not before Derek had recognized it.

Replacing the lid of the box and clambering after it, Derek saw the doll had returned to the cellar of the doll's house and to the tightly packed coffins. Forcing himself, Derek slid open one of the coffins and discovered inside a female. She was heavy, and when he shook her he could hear the liquid inside moving. A convenient container, he suddenly realized, for a blind vampire who could no longer fend for himself.

The miniature vampire stared up at him, dark eyes full of hatred, and then scuttled towards him like a spider. Derek rapidly closed up the house and slid back the roof. The squeaking dimmed as Derek remembered Mrs Cole's translation of the label.

More dimly he could also remember his uncle saying,

'I'm stuck with it now. Can't sell it. That wouldn't be right.'

How long would the blind vampire be sustained by the dolls? When would he need fresh supplies? Presumably they had lasted a good long time. Or was his miniature assistant somehow getting out of the shop and refilling his cup? Or had sorcery been used and, like an everlasting spring, would the dolls always be magically replenished?

As he hurried towards the door and hastily locked up, Derek knew he would never dare to enter his uncle's toy shop again. Looking up at the faded shop sign, he heard a noise behind him and he saw his father standing there. As Derek began to make flustered excuses, his father waved them aside.

'I understand,' he said. 'He had a fascinating collection. But I've managed to break the will and we're going to sell the shop at last. So I thought I'd do a quick stock-take.' He opened the door with his new set of keys and disappeared inside.

Derek was about to warn him, when he realized he wouldn't be believed. He wondered how soon they'd find out . . .

Colin turned to Jodie, who appeared to be listening intently, but not to him.

'Aren't those footsteps?' she whispered.

Jon got up in a panic and someone gave a little scream.

They all froze. Then a familiar figure appeared.

'It's the warden,' said Jodie with relief.

'What are you lot doing down here?' he asked angrily. 'You know I said the crypt was out of bounds. You don't have to rush away though,' he added persuasively. 'Not now.'

The warden smiled, showing his teeth.

DEAD MAN AT THE DOOR

Gary and his family are newcomers to the Isle of Wight but Gary is soon to find his life inextricably bound up with both the island and the supernatural.

'A truly terrifying story' – *Sunday Telegraph*

HORROR STORIES TO TELL IN THE DARK

Especially for those who don't find scary stories frightening enough, here is an excellent collection of horror stories to read after lights out.

TRAVELLERS' TALES

The Roberts family are Romany travellers, born and bred, but the traditional pattern of their lives is changing and their treasured right to roam is threatened. This is the moving story of a family fighting to preserve its individuality.